"Tessie likes you."

"She's special, isn't she?" Gracie replied.

"You're my first choice to help me take care of her," Calen replied.

Gracie smiled and nodded. "I'm glad to help, then."

Calen draped a blanket over Gracie's shoulders and tucked it between them in the place under his arm where she was pressed against him. She closed her eyes as though she was weary.

Then he leaned over and kissed her forehead.

"What's that for?" she muttered sleepily.

He smiled. "Nothing."

"You always were a Romeo," she whispered without opening her eyes. "A woman in every port, Buck used to say."

"I never did take to the sea," he corrected her mildly. He wondered suddenly how different their futures would have been if he'd been the first one to ask Gracie out on a date in high school. He had wanted to, but his nerves had failed him. By the time he got the courage, Buck had asked her instead.

Maybe there was time yet to find out where the feelings he had for her would lead if he let them….

Books by Janet Tronstad

Love Inspired

*An Angel for Dry Creek
*A Gentleman for Dry Creek
*A Bride for Dry Creek
*A Rich Man for Dry Creek
*A Hero for Dry Creek
*A Baby for Dry Creek
*A Dry Creek Christmas
*Sugar Plums for Dry Creek
*At Home in Dry Creek
†The Sisterhood of the
  Dropped Stitches
*A Match Made in Dry Creek
*Shepherds Abiding in
  Dry Creek
†A Dropped Stitches Christmas
*Dry Creek Sweethearts
†A Heart for the
  Dropped Stitches
*A Dry Creek Courtship
*Snowbound in Dry Creek
†A Dropped Stitches Wedding
*Small-Town Brides
  "A Dry Creek Wedding"

*Silent Night in Dry Creek
*Wife Wanted in Dry Creek
  Doctor Right
*Small-Town Moms
  "A Dry Creek Family"
**Sleigh Bells for Dry Creek
**Lilac Wedding in Dry Creek
**Wildflower Bride in
  Dry Creek
**Second Chance in
  Dry Creek

Love Inspired Historical

*Calico Christmas at
  Dry Creek
*Mistletoe Courtship
  "Christmas Bells for
  Dry Creek"
  Mail-Order Christmas Brides
  "Christmas Stars for
  Dry Creek"

*Dry Creek
†Dropped Stitches
**Return to Dry Creek

JANET TRONSTAD

grew up on her family's farm in central Montana and now lives in Pasadena, California, where she is always at work on her next book. She has written more than thirty books, many of them set in the fictitious town of Dry Creek, Montana, where the men spend the winters gathered around the potbellied stove in the hardware store and the women make jelly in the fall.

Second Chance in Dry Creek

Janet Tronstad

Recycling programs
for this product may
not exist in your area.

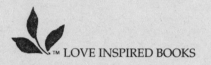

™ LOVE INSPIRED BOOKS

ISBN-13: 978-0-373-81648-4

SECOND CHANCE IN DRY CREEK

Copyright © 2012 by Janet Tronstad

www.LoveInspiredBooks.com

Printed in U.S.A.

He causes His sun to rise on the wicked
and the good, and He makes it rain on the just
and the unjust.
—*Matthew* 5:45

I dedicate this book to broken families.
May God have mercy on all of us.

Chapter One

Gracie Stone sat at the kitchen table, a cup of tea growing cold in front of her. She gathered her frayed bathrobe around her against the night's chill and glanced up at the clock, wincing when she saw it was almost midnight. Every time she was ready to doze off, she remembered the determined voices of her grown sons as they had vowed earlier in the day that they were going to find a husband for her.

"They're just worried about me living alone," she muttered to Rusty, the dog lying at her feet. There had been a string of gas station robberies up north around Havre, and she supposed the boys were right to be concerned.

"But a husband? That's a bit extreme," she said, telling her faithful companion the same thing she'd told her sons, as she bent down to rub the dog's ears. She had returned to the family ranch in Dry Creek, Montana, to get her old life back, not start a new one. "They should know I'm not going to take a chance on marriage again."

Suddenly, a flicker of light shone briefly through the window above the sink.

Gracie blinked before realizing it had to be the headlights of a vehicle driving over the small rise in the lane that led to her house. She figured she might as well put the teakettle back on the burner. As she stood up, she wondered which of her three sons had looked out his window in the middle of the night and noticed that her light was on. Each lived with his newlywed wife on the ranch property, their individual houses just far apart enough to need separate driveways.

Gracie reached up to the cupboard for another mug. She would appreciate the company tonight even if she had to listen to another lecture on the virtues of matrimony. Rusty seemed to agree. He'd gotten to his feet and was running in circles around the table, barking as he went.

"Hush now," she said. The dog was always excited to see her sons.

Just then, she heard the sound of the engine stopping. Shortly thereafter she heard a faint knock on her kitchen door.

She paused, the mug still in her hand. She hadn't heard footsteps on the porch, and all of her sons wore cowboy boots that beat a loud rhythm as they pounded up those old wooden steps. Rusty usually didn't carry on for this long when they came, either.

"Just a minute," she called as she set the cup down on the counter and tightened the sash on her robe. Her feet were bare, but that couldn't be helped. At least she was wearing an old T-shirt and sweatpants under her robe.

She stepped over to the sink and looked through the window. The porch was around the corner, but she could see a small car, its headlights still on, parked in her driveway. She didn't recognize the vehicle, but then none of the neighbors would be knocking at her door at this time of night without phoning first anyway.

"Yes?" she said as she walked closer to the door.

Her youngest son, Tyler, had called a few hours ago to make sure she had locked both doors before going to bed, and she was glad she had followed his advice. The October night was darker than usual, so she assumed the clouds were still overhead. The stars were hidden and winter was forecast to come early this year. Tonight was already cold.

She didn't hear anything for a minute. Rusty had stopped barking, but he walked over to the door and growled low in his throat.

"I need—" a woman started, her voice so soft Gracie couldn't hear more than that even though she had been leaning close to the door.

Gracie breathed a sigh of relief. The robberies had been committed by two men in black ski masks. There'd been no mention of a woman. Rusty's growl faded, and that meant he was satisfied with whoever was on the other side of the door.

Still, Gracie figured she needed to show some caution.

"Where are you headed?" she asked. Anyone who was lost on these gravel roads wouldn't be able to find their way in the dark; that much she knew. Half of these old roads weren't even marked. And there were no lights, of course.

"Calen Gray," the woman said, her voice falling with each syllable as though her strength was draining away.

"Calen?" Gracie repeated in surprise. He was the foreman of the nearby Elkton Ranch and was in church most Sundays, even though she seldom greeted him. She never knew what to say; he'd seen her and her late husband at their worst years ago, and there were some things she preferred to forget. She expected he felt the same way.

Gracie was reaching for the doorknob when she heard a soft thud.

Dear Lord, what is wrong? She prayed for guidance as she turned the lock. She opened the door slowly and stared into the darkness. The light from her kitchen was weak. The headlights from the car lit up the yard, but the partially-enclosed porch stayed in shadows.

Gracie heard a moan and looked down to her right. The woman must have tried to steady herself on the wooden cabinet before crumpling to the slatted floor next to it. Rusty had slipped out of the house and was sniffing around her.

"Are you all right?" Gracie asked softly as she knelt down and motioned for Rusty to back away. The young woman's denim-clad legs were at an awkward angle. Her skin was clammy as Gracie touched her face. There was not even a murmur in response. Gracie looked closer and brushed aside the woman's brown hair. That's when she saw a dark bruise above the woman's eye. Another faded one showed on her cheek.

Gracie recognized discolorations like that, and her lips tightened. Someone had hit this young woman recently and not for the first time.

"She might not even be out of high school," Gracie looked up and muttered to Rusty. He looked over in sympathy, but obediently kept to the edge of the steps.

Fortunately, the new wall phone her sons had installed was close to the door, and Gracie only needed to stand and reach through the opening to pull the phone to her. She called Tyler, since he'd had some medical training in the military.

"I need your help," Gracie said when her son answered. "A woman passed out on the porch and she's—"

"I'll be right there," he said. Then he hung up.

Gracie nodded even though Tyler couldn't see her. He kept a first aid bag near his back door and he'd bring it along.

The woman stirred again. Gracie thought maybe Rusty made her uncomfortable, but when the woman opened her eyes and glanced around frantically, she didn't even pause as she glanced at the dog. Gracie knew it was more than that.

"It's just my son coming over," Gracie murmured, but that didn't seem to soothe the woman. "He's one of the good guys. You're safe here. No one will hurt you."

So it was a man she feared, Gracie thought to herself.

The woman's eyes closed again, although her breath was still ragged.

Gracie realized she continued to hold the phone in her hand. She punched in another number, one she had memorized years ago when she'd thought she might need this kind of help herself. She'd longed for a friend back then almost as much as she did now. Her husband had kept her so isolated. But she'd never called the number until now.

"Calen?"

She had no sooner said his name than she realized she did not know him well enough these days to trust him. He'd given her that number almost twenty years ago. He might go to church now, but she didn't really know that he was safe.

"Gracie?"

"I'm sorry—I—"

The woman moaned.

"I dialed the wrong number," Gracie said, even though she knew it made no sense. She disconnected the call and set the phone down on the floor of the porch. It had been so long since she'd been in an abusive relationship that she had forgotten the first rule of protection. Never assume that a man is innocent just because he seems nice on the surface. No one, except her teenage sons, had known her husband was severely beating her all those years ago.

She reached over to reassure the woman. By that time, a strong beam from approaching headlights flickered through the screen on the porch. Rusty moved in closer and gave a quick yip.

"My son's here," Gracie murmured, and left her hand on the woman's shoulder. "He'll be able to help you."

The woman seemed fragile and that only made Gracie want to protect her more. She'd been blessed with sons, but had always wanted a daughter, too.

She wondered what Calen's relationship was to this stranger. He never asked for prayers for himself in church, so she had no idea what his life was like. But then, she never asked for prayers, either. She preferred to keep her business to herself, so she couldn't fault him for doing the same. Still, it made her uneasy. She'd never figured Calen for the kind of man who would get involved with a woman so much younger than himself.

It was a pity really, because apart from that Calen was—

She'd scarcely started that thought when she stopped. Maybe her sons were more astute than she had realized. She might not trust any man enough to marry him, but she suddenly wished she could. Not that it would be Calen, of course. They had too much history. But sometimes, like now, she missed having a man at her side. She'd had a miserable marriage, yet she still believed a couple could live happily ever after if they loved each other enough.

She shook her head at her own foolishness and took a long look at the bruises on the woman in front of her. That should be reminder enough. Some women didn't get a happily ever after. They got a nightmare instead. She wondered if the young woman still dreamed of true love and if she thought she'd found it with a ranch foreman who had to be twice her age.

Calen sat in his bedroom in the Elkton bunkhouse and stared at the phone in his hand. The darkness outside his window was deep and the night was silent. He'd heard the panic in Gracie's voice. And he didn't believe she had dialed his number by mistake.

Without thinking, he swung his legs out of

bed. It would only take him a couple of minutes to go to her place and check on her. He had failed to help her when she'd needed him more than a decade ago; he wasn't going to let her down again.

He barely had time to pray for every worry that raced through his mind before he pulled into the driveway that led to the main Stone ranch house. As he sped over the small rise, he could see a car and two pickups parked near the porch.

Calen pulled his pickup to a stop behind the last vehicle and started walking over to the porch. A dog turned and growled at him, but Calen didn't hesitate. He was prepared to knock on Gracie's kitchen door, but there was no need. The door was wide open, even though two people were kneeling in the shadows.

"What's wrong?" he said as he took the steps up to the porch.

"I shouldn't have called you," Gracie said as she looked up. He didn't think she was really aware of him until he spoke.

"Please leave," she added. "Everything's fine."

Gracie's long black hair was pulled into a braid that ran down her back. She always had been a striking woman, and her Cherokee ancestry was pronounced in the shadows. Dark brown eyes were cold as she looked at him. Her fine-boned hands gripped the collar of her cotton robe with enough strength to betray her agitation, even though her face told him absolutely nothing of her thoughts.

"I'm not going to leave until you tell me what's wrong." He was relieved to see that Gracie's youngest son, Tyler, was the other person kneeling there. The two of them had fished together many years ago. Even as a boy, he'd always had good sense.

"We have a bit of a situation here," Tyler answered, lifting his head.

"Someone has been beating up on this woman," Gracie interrupted fiercely, her emotions breaking through now and her eyes flashing as they met Calen's. "And it's not going to happen again."

He couldn't miss her meaning. "I've never hit a woman in my life."

Did she really think that of him? he wondered in dismay.

"You and my husband grew up together," she continued bitterly. "You were best friends. I had forgotten that until now."

Calen felt the guilt twist inside of him. He didn't know how he hadn't seen that abusive side of Buck Stone. "If I had known what was happening in this house, I would have done something. You have to believe that."

Gracie was silent. They'd both gone through some rough times, Calen told himself. He was forty-eight years old now. She was a year younger. Maybe if he hadn't been so strongly attracted to her when she'd moved to Dry Creek back in high school, he would have kept hanging out with Buck after he'd married her. Maybe then he would have seen the changes in the man.

"We need to call the sheriff." Tyler spoke without looking up from the woman.

"What?" Gracie and Calen said in unison as they turned to stare at him.

"Someone may have been beating up on her," Tyler explained. "But the reason she passed out is that she's been shot. It's more of a graze than anything, but she has been slowly losing blood."

Tyler shifted his position as he held up a hand with a small spot of red. When he moved, Calen was finally able to see the face of the woman lying on the porch.

"Renee?" he whispered.

"You know her?" Gracie asked. Her tone was flat, and she didn't give away her feelings even though he sensed she disapproved.

Calen turned to look at her squarely. "Renee is my daughter."

A wave of shock flashed across Gracie's face. Her skin paled and her lips parted as if she was going to say something, but couldn't think of the words. If they'd talked about anything important in the past decade, he would have mentioned his daughter to her. He wondered if Buck had even told her about his brief marriage to Renee's mother.

"Tell the sheriff we need an ambulance," Tyler said as he picked up the phone lying on the porch and handed it to Calen. "Your Renee put some kind of bandage on the wound herself, but it didn't work. The sooner we get her to an emergency room, the better."

Calen took the phone as Tyler turned back to his patient.

"I could use some clean water," Tyler said without looking up.

"I'll get it." Gracie stood.

Calen dialed the sheriff's number as he moved slightly so he could see Renee's face better. What kind of trouble had his daughter gotten herself into? He'd married her mother on the rebound when he'd gotten her pregnant, even though he was still half in love with Gracie. The marriage had been doomed from the start and he'd been too young and inexperienced to save it. Finally, his wife had left him, telling him she preferred to get child support instead of being stuck on a ranch in the middle of nowhere with a squalling baby and a man who smelled like horses. Nothing he'd said had prevented her from leaving. It had all happened two decades ago, but when he turned to God several years back, it was the one thing he'd needed forgiveness for the most. He wasn't sure he'd tried hard enough to save his marriage, and he had lost his daughter in the process.

"Sheriff Wall? Could you come out to the Stone place?"

The last time Calen had seen his daughter was five years ago. He remembered that time better than he did the days of his marriage. Renee had spent several happy weeks with him on the Elkton Ranch. She'd gone back to her mother's home in Seattle after that, only to run away two years later. He'd tried to find her, but she hadn't left any trail.

Gracie stepped back through the open door as Calen ended the call with the sheriff. She held a steel pan filled with steaming water. A white dish towel was draped over her shoulder.

"I took the water from the teakettle," Gracie said as she set the pan down on the porch and then handed the towel to Tyler. "So it's boiled."

"Thanks," Tyler said as he dipped the towel in the water. "I want to get the wound cleaned up. I don't know what she used to bandage it. It's hard to see anything with her jacket on."

Tyler was removing the jacket as he spoke.

"I can boil more water if you need," Gracie said.

"I don't—" Tyler began and then stopped. He unwrapped the bandage and pulled something out. "This is what she used to try and stop the bleeding."

The faint light barely showed what it was, and it took them all a moment to see it clearly.

"A black ski mask," Calen said finally, the bleakness in his voice thick enough to be heard by everyone on the porch.

Renee moaned. Calen wondered if she could hear them speaking.

Gracie made a sound of sympathy and, to his surprise, stepped closer and put a hand on his arm.

"It doesn't need to mean anything," she said softly.

Calen looked down at her. "Innocent until proven guilty, is that it?"

She nodded and he wondered if she understood the irony of it all. Gracie had served almost ten years in prison because no one had questioned her confession that she had murdered her abusive husband. People assumed she had reached her limit and snapped. No one realized she'd believed, incorrectly, that one of her sons was guilty. She had done it to spare her children.

And now she was trying to spare his child. And he was the one who should have known Gracie would never harm anyone. Back then, she had too much pride to ask for help, but he should have realized what she was doing. It wasn't the only time he had let her down in the past, and he'd be surprised if she didn't remember his failures every time she looked at his weather-beaten face.

He saw a flash of red lights then. The sheriff wouldn't come in with his siren going, but he used the lights at night when it was an emergency.

For the first time, Calen understood Gracie's urge to save her sons from the law. He felt the same way about Renee. He might have made his share of mistakes in life, but he didn't want Renee to suffer for hers. He'd take the punishment himself if he could.

Lord, what is that daughter of mine mixed up in? Calen prayed silently. Why hadn't Renee sent him word when she'd left her mother's place? He would have driven anywhere to pick her up and bring her home with him. He had saved money for a down payment on a ranch of his own, but he had stopped looking for property. He wanted to have the cash to pay the investigators if they ever picked up a lead on Renee. Now it seemed that he might need his seventy thousand dollars for a defense attorney instead.

He sensed Gracie standing straight beside him even though his eyes were on Sheriff Carl Wall stepping out of his county car. Now that Calen had come to terms with what was happening, he wished it wasn't Gracie standing next to him. He never had managed to look good in her eyes and, while he'd made his peace with that, he still wished he could stand tall when he was next to her. A man needed to have some pride around a woman he had once loved, especially when the woman had never really noticed his existence. He only hoped things didn't get any worse—and that, if they did, Gracie wasn't standing beside him to see it all.

Chapter Two

Gracie watched the sheriff step up onto the porch. He wasn't wearing his uniform and looked as if he'd grabbed the closest jeans and sweatshirt he could find to put on his large frame. The man's face was plain, but his heart was good and Gracie was glad he was here.

"What's wrong?" the lawman asked, peering into the shadows.

The headlights were still on in Renee's car and Rusty had gone over there to race around that vehicle for a change.

"We have a woman who's been hurt," Gracie said. A nudge would be all it should take for the sheriff to know that the priority was to treat Renee's wounds. Any questions about that ski mask could wait.

"She's lost a fair amount of blood," Tyler added.

"Any reason we can't move her?" the sheriff asked, as he crouched down beside her.

"No broken bones as far as I can tell," Tyler noted as he looked Renee over. "She'd ride more comfortably in the ambulance if there's one on the way out from Miles City."

"It should be here in a few minutes," the sheriff said, as he stood back up and looked around. "Any idea what happened?"

Gracie tried to keep her eyes off Calen, but she didn't succeed. Shadows hid his face and a muscle flexed in his jaw. His brown hair hadn't been combed, falling forward as he looked down at his daughter. She'd always thought he was one of those charming men who waltzed through life with no troubles. Her husband used to say Calen never turned down a chance to party, and that's why Buck had claimed he'd stopped hanging out with him after they were married. But Calen wasn't having a good time tonight. Strangely enough, the worry in his eyes made him more handsome than she remembered.

"We found a black ski mask on her," Calen finally said, his voice flat as he looked up and faced the sheriff resolutely.

The lawman grunted in surprise. "I got a message that they'd arrested one of the thieves tonight. The other one got away. The fools tried to rob that gas station between Havre and Malta. The owner is ex-military and he had a gun behind the counter. Used it, too."

"I thought they were looking for two men," Gracie reminded everyone. "A gunshot wound doesn't mean a crime has been committed."

She knew all about the mistakes that could be made in the legal system, and she didn't want this young woman to suffer through an arrest if she was innocent.

The sheriff shrugged. "Maybe the other one did all the talking. With a ski mask, the second one could have been a woman, if she was slight. Besides, what other reason does she have for being in this area?"

"She's my daughter," Calen said. "She was coming to see me."

Gracie noticed that stopped the sheriff for a moment. "Not little Renee? I remember her riding that horse you had. She wasn't more than twelve or so."

The sheriff looked down at the young woman as though trying to see traces of the child she had been. Gracie wished she'd taken a minute to wash the grime off the woman's face. She looked like a pixie who had fallen out of a tree, all bruises and smudges and torn clothes.

"She was fourteen when she was here last,"

Calen continued after a moment, his voice strained. "Sixteen when she ran away from her mother's home. That'd make her nineteen now, almost twenty. She's always been small for her age. Any trouble she's in is my fault. I should have made her mother send her to me. Those weeks she spent with me on the Elkton Ranch were all I had. She's a good kid. Maybe a little wild, but she needed her father and I wasn't there for her."

Gracie watched Calen stumble to a halt. She had always assumed he had no deep sorrows in life. She knew tonight that she'd been wrong.

"You can't argue with the courts in those custody battles," the sheriff said as he stood up. "Back then they almost always gave it to the mother. There wasn't much you could have done."

Gracie saw another flash of headlights coming down the road to her house. "That must be the ambulance now."

They were all silent as the ambulance came close to the house and parked with the other vehicles. Two male paramedics jumped out almost before the driver had stopped. Renee made a soft sound, and Gracie figured the pounding of their footsteps had reached her unconscious.

Tyler and the sheriff stepped aside as the

paramedics both knelt down, one reaching out to take her pulse and the other feeling for broken bones.

"She's got a gunshot wound in the side," Tyler said from the corner where he stood.

The paramedic taking the pulse looked up at the sheriff.

The lawman shrugged. "Medical problems take precedent. We don't know for sure how she got shot." He looked at Gracie as he talked to the young men. "A gunshot wound does not prove a crime has actually taken place."

The other paramedic was removing Renee's shoes when she winced and seemed to wake up a bit more.

"Looks like a sprain, too," he said.

"I'll get the stretcher," the other paramedic said.

Gracie took a step closer to Renee and knelt down again, reaching over to brush the brown hair back from her face. Her eyes fluttered open and, again, the night deepened their searching violet color.

"These men are going to help you," Gracie said, trying to gauge whether her words were penetrating. "The ambulance will take you to a clinic where they can get you all fixed up."

"No," the young woman gasped, as she

looked around frantically and tried to sit up. "I can't—"

Calen knelt on the other side of her, and it did not take long for Renee to see him. Her eyes focused on him and she quieted down. "Daddy?"

She lay back down.

"I'm here," Calen said as he touched her shoulder.

"Please," Renee said, and then gulped. "Please—Tessie—"

"I'll do whatever I can to help you," Calen pledged, his voice filled with emotion. "I don't know about your partner, but—"

By that time, the paramedics were back. "Excuse us."

Gracie and Calen both stood and moved so the men would have room to load Renee onto the stretcher. Just the lifting seemed too much and she passed out again. The driver of the ambulance had backed the vehicle as close to the steps as possible.

"If I get my hands on that Tessie of hers, I'll give him a piece of my mind," Calen muttered, his voice so low only Gracie would hear him. "What kind of a grown man goes by Tessie anyway?"

He turned then and Gracie put her hand on his arm. "Renee is probably in shock. She might not even know what she is saying. Tessie could be anyone."

The two paramedics carried the stretcher down the steps toward the open door of the vehicle.

Calen followed them off the porch and to the rear of the ambulance as they were loading his daughter. "I'm going to follow along behind you."

"I'll be there, too," the sheriff said as he stood at the base of the steps. "Keep a good eye on her."

"Give us a few minutes first," one of the paramedics said before he climbed into the ambulance behind his partner. The driver put the vehicle in gear. "It'll take some time to get her unloaded and triaged. No point in you getting there before that."

The paramedic closed the door. Calen walked back to the porch and stood by Gracie.

Together they watched the vehicle turn around and start down the lane, carrying his daughter. Gracie knew he was distressed, but she couldn't think of any words to ease his troubles.

"They'll take good care of her in Miles City," she finally said.

She knew what it was like to see a child suffer and not be able to do anything about it.

She glanced sideways and saw the shadows on Calen's face. "I'm sorry."

Her words made him flinch and Gracie knew she'd made a mistake. She wasn't offering pity, but it likely sounded that way. Another apology wouldn't help anything though, so she turned to go back into the house. She had forgotten that darkness made strangers into friends too quickly. Calen probably already regretted sharing his troubles with her, and she didn't intend to force him.

Tyler stepped closer to the steps, and Rusty ran back to sniff his boots. Gracie had not yet reached the door to the house when she heard the dog and turned around.

"Rusty is sure wound up," Tyler said as he crouched to greet the canine, then glanced up at Gracie before looking down again. "Are you still keeping him inside at night? Remember, he's a barn dog. Always has been. He needs to be where he can get out and run if he wants."

Tyler paused a moment as though suddenly unsure of himself. The light from the house shone softly on his face as he looked at his mother. "It's not like you to need him inside. Do you? You sure you're all right?" He hesitated. "You could come spend your nights at our place if you'd sleep better. Angelina would love to have you with us. And you know we've got plenty of room."

"You also have that security system that rivals Fort Knox—" Gracie said. "I'm afraid I'd make the alarm go off if I got up in the middle of the night to get a drink of water."

"That was Angelina's father's idea," Tyler protested. "You know he's used to living in a big city where that kind of thing is common. We don't even turn the alarm on half the time."

"Well, I sleep just fine where I am," Gracie said before she realized it wasn't true. "Well, usually."

She stepped over and knelt down to give her dog another rub on its back. He was better than any expensive security system. And it was nobody's business if she wanted him inside at night. She didn't want to intrude on her sons' lives. She loved her daughters-in-law, each one of them, but she felt a new bride needed time to set up her home without a mother-in-law sleeping over every night. It was enough that they all got together on Sundays after church for dinner. That was her time.

"That's quite the guard dog you have there," the sheriff said as he came back to the porch and bent down to pet Rusty, too. The canine responded by increasing his barking.

Gracie thought Rusty was showing off, begging for more attention, and she was happy for him to get it. He was a good dog.

"He wants to show us something," Calen finally said as he studied the animal. "He likely won't stop until we see what it is, even if it's just an old bone he found."

"Rusty?" Gracie asked from where she was kneeling on the cold boards of the porch, resting her hand on the dog's back. She had meant it as a question, but Rusty took it as approval and ran over to Renee's car again. This time his barking sounded urgent to Gracie, too.

"What in the world?" Tyler said as he stood up and started following the sheriff toward the car.

Gracie started to stand up, but her knee was suddenly locked. She had a touch of arthritis in her joints that had started giving her trouble this past summer, but usually it was nothing like this. It was the price of getting older, she told herself as she waited for the stiffness to pass. It also came from her winters spent in a cold cell, but she didn't like to remember that.

Unfortunately, Calen had stayed back while the other two men followed the dog.

She had bitten back the initial groan, but she must have signaled something was wrong with an indrawn breath, because he studied her.

"Can I help you?" He finally stepped close and offered Gracie a hand. She looked up. He was in the shadows, but she could see the concern on his face.

She wanted to refuse. She could take care of herself. But it seemed churlish to protest, so she nodded and accepted the calloused hand he offered.

"Thank you," she said as she stood. The sash was loose on her robe and she knotted it securely. Even with the T-shirt and sweatpants she wore, she felt self-conscious. When she'd first stepped out on the porch, she had been warm enough, but she was shivering now.

"You don't have any shoes on," Calen said as though he'd suddenly noticed. "Can I go inside and get some shoes—or at least some slippers—for you?"

The thought of Calen finding her pink slippers next to her bed made her blush as much as her Cherokee coloring would allow. "I walk barefoot sometimes. It's okay. I'm fine."

Her great-grandfather had been a chief. She was not a delicate flower.

Calen frowned. "Your teeth are chattering—"

"Hey, come over here." Tyler interrupted them from where he stood beside Renee's car. The sheriff was looking in the window to the backseat.

Gracie heard a soft keening then, almost like a sound Rusty would make. But the dog was standing quietly by the car. Gracie had a bad feeling about that sound. Some animal was terrified.

Without thinking, Gracie started down the steps. And then drew in her breath sharply when her feet met the hard ground. Calen had been right. This ground would be covered with frost by morning. Winter would be here in a few days—before the church's harvest dinner could mark the change of season. And her feet were not up to this.

She almost turned back, but she heard the keening again.

"Allow me," Calen said as he stepped closer. He hesitated for a moment, standing next to her in the darkness. Then he reached down and scooped her up as easily as he'd lift a bale of hay.

Gracie gasped. She certainly hadn't expected that.

Before she knew it, Calen was carrying her over to the car as though she was weightless. Her stomach felt light enough for it to be true. She wasn't used to being this close to a man. And he smelled like soap and forest pine. In the places where her cheek touched his shoulder, she could feel his muscles moving. Her bare feet dangled as he walked. She glanced up to ask him to set her down because she felt disoriented, but she stopped when she saw the set lines of his face.

He seemed so focused on getting to the car that she figured he was carrying her as an efficiency—which made her hesitate. She didn't want to protest as though she thought it was some grand, romantic gesture when it was only a practical matter. She glanced up at him again and noticed his lips were pressed even tighter together. No, she told herself, it definitely wasn't a romantic gesture.

Calen barely kept from grinding his teeth. He used to dream of picking Gracie up like this and, now that he had done it, he wondered where his good sense had gone. He wasn't gaining any points with her—that much was clear. He could feel the protest almost bursting out of her, so he walked a little faster. Besides, he didn't have time for old high school dreams. He needed to concentrate on the present right now so he could help his daughter.

"Don't tell me she left the money from the robberies in the car?" Calen said to no one in particular as he got closer to where the sheriff stood. Of course, having the money might be a good thing, he reminded himself. At least Renee could give it back. That might gain her some leniency with the judge when she went to trial. He had heard the news reports about the robberies up north, but it never crossed his mind that Renee might be involved.

Calen set Gracie on the trunk of the car. She didn't even meet his eyes, and he figured that couldn't be good. So he looked away and saw Tyler.

"It's not the money," Tyler said once he had Calen's attention.

If Calen hadn't been in such a hurry, he might have wondered why Tyler's voice had become softer as he stood there, the door to the backseat open.

Calen moved closer. The overhead light in the car gave off a dim glow, but he had no trouble seeing the beige cloth upholstery. A brown paper bag sat in the far corner with a plastic bread wrapper sticking up. A child's car seat sat next to a red vinyl suitcase. If he wasn't mistaken, he smelled fried chicken, likely the kind found at truck stops. He had to lean into the car before he could see the bundle of blankets on the floorboards and, even then, he took another moment to realize what it was.

"A little girl?" Calen whispered, fearful that Renee might have kidnapped a child somewhere in her flight. He wasn't even sure if it was a girl. All he saw was a swatch of curly blond hair peeking out from the top of the blankets.

But then the keening sounded again and it was decidedly feminine.

"Are you okay?" Calen said then, bending down so he could see further into the car. For a moment, it didn't matter who the girl was, she was terrified and he wanted to soothe her.

The blankets dipped slightly and he saw two tearful blue eyes peeking out. Calen knew the moment she saw him, as the sound she was making turned to a shriek and the blanket covered her eyes again.

Calen backed out of the car.

"I don't want to scare her," he said. Gracie had slid down from the trunk and was standing beside Tyler. Both of them had frowns on their faces. The sheriff had a flashlight and was shining the beam into the front seat of the car.

"I think I have something," the lawman said as he opened that door.

The sheriff reached inside and pulled out a white envelope, squinting at it in the soft light of the car, and then looked at Calen. "It's got your name on it."

The man handed the letter to him. "I hope this gives us some answers. I haven't received any alerts about missing children, but she might have been snatched tonight and not listed as missing yet."

"Oh, I can't believe Renee would kidnap some poor child," Gracie burst out with a protest and gathered the collar of her robe more tightly around her. "She doesn't look like she's much more than a child herself."

Calen glanced over and gave her a grateful smile before looking down. In her bathrobe, Gracie didn't look that much older than Renee.

"Here," he said with a gesture to the open door of the backseat. "You may as well sit inside the car. The child is going to need to talk to someone before long anyway."

Calen bowed his head, holding the envelope. *Father, give me wisdom for anything I read. Be with my daughter and the child in the car. Protect them both. Amen.*

As he pulled the envelope flap back, Calen noticed how quiet it was. He glanced into the car again and saw that the girl had crawled up into Gracie's lap. The little one still had tear streaks on her cheeks, but she looked calm for the first time. Maybe they'd be able to get some answers after all.

The envelope started to feel heavy in his hands. What had Renee wanted to say to him after all these years anyway?

Chapter Three

Gracie felt the girl snuggle as close as she could to her in the backseat of the car. Even then, the poor thing was shivering, and Gracie didn't think it was from the cold alone because the girl had the blanket wrapped around her when she climbed over to Gracie.

"What's your name?" Gracie whispered as she put her hand on the child's head in much the same way as she soothed Rusty. She'd guess the child was two, maybe three years old.

The girl looked up at her, her eyes filling with tears.

Gracie felt her start to tremble more and she drew the little one closer to her. "That's all right. You don't need to talk right now. We'll figure it out later."

The words soothed the girl and she nestled

back against Gracie, drawing the blanket over her head.

Gracie wished, and not for the first time since she had come back to Dry Creek, that she was more accepted in this community. She'd have more to offer this little one if she could call up a neighbor and ask how to help her talk. Her sons thought she needed a husband, but what she really needed was friends. The young mothers at church led their children away when she came near, and conversations stopped when she entered a room. She understood, of course. No one knew what to say to her now that she was an ex-con and, no matter how much she tried, she couldn't seem to make it any better.

Mrs. Hargrove and her husband, Charley, accepted her, of course, but they were more like a kindly aunt and uncle than friends. For almost a year, Gracie had hid from what was happening, just as this little girl was doing now with her blanket. It was time to pull the covering away from her eyes and admit that she might never be accepted in this community. The people here acted like prison was a germ they could catch by being near her, and that was foolish. But they were right that she was different from them in ways they might find impossible to ever accept.

Looking down, she gently wiped the tears off the girl's cheek. Gracie might not know as much about little girls as the women in the church did, but she knew how this poor child felt. Prison had taught her one thing. She recognized fear when she saw it.

After the child was breathing deeply in sleep, Gracie looked back at the men standing just outside the car. They had been watching her and the girl. Gracie shook her head slightly at them to show she knew nothing more than they did.

After a minute or so had passed in silence, Calen pulled the single sheet of paper out of the envelope and unfolded it.

Gracie could see it was written in pencil, and Calen squinted, probably having a hard time making out the faint letters in the wan light coming from the interior of the car. Then the sheriff stepped over with his flashlight and shone the beam on the letter.

"Oh." Calen pulled back at the sudden light. Then, he began to read.

"Dad." He cleared his throat, his voice heavy with an emotion that made Gracie blink back tears. A good parent always wanted to protect their child. She looked down at the little girl she held, thinking of how forlorn her sons must have been when she was in prison.

She had missed them. During those years, seeing women grieve for the lost time with their children forged her strongest bond with the others, especially when she realized that their grief, like hers, was filled with guilt as well.

"Dad," Calen began to read the letter again. "I'm in trouble and I don't have anyone to take care of Tessie, my daughter—"

Calen broke off reading and looked over to where Gracie held the girl.

"This must be Tessie," he whispered in wonder.

Gracie nodded. She saw the hope in Calen's face. His whole face changed when he realized the girl was his daughter's child. His mouth relaxed, his eyes lifted in a smile.

"Well, what do you know?" the sheriff said then as he looked at Calen. "You're a grandpa. What else does your daughter say?"

Calen looked back at the letter. He sounded eager now. "It says here that Tessie is a special child, and Renee doesn't want her to go into the foster-care system if something happens."

Calen paused at that and looked at the sheriff. "Is that what they'll do? Send her away?"

The sheriff thought a minute. "I need to call family services in when I arrest someone and they have a child with them. Of course, until the arrest, I don't have much need to. As long as I know the child's safe."

"You can't let Tessie go into the foster-care system," Gracie protested. "The poor thing is terrified already."

She could feel how fragile the child was.

"Foster care is no place for a toddler," Tyler added as he stepped around the sheriff and moved closer to the car. His voice challenged the lawman.

"I don't know what the courts will do," the sheriff said defensively. "But sometimes foster care is for the best."

"No, it's not," Tyler said swiftly. "Not by a long shot."

Gracie's heart broke. Her two youngest sons had never complained to her about being sent to that state home when she went to prison, but she knew in that instant she could never do enough to make it up to them.

She looked up at Tyler. The light from the sheriff's flashlight was directed at the letter in Calen's hands, but it caught the expression on Tyler's face as well. He was looking at the girl in her arms as if he dared anyone to take the child away.

Gracie forced herself to remain calm. Tessie was still asleep, her head lying on Gracie's shoulder. She looked up then and saw the ranch foreman staring at them.

"I suppose you think I let my sons down, too," Gracie said to Calen.

"I'm not one to judge," he said.

Calen had too much pride to beg, either. He'd been bucked off a horse once, but he had walked back to camp without asking for help even though his leg bone was splintered. Seeing Gracie with his new granddaughter made him want to fall to his knees and plead with her to tell him what she had done to give peace to the girl.

"Tessie will live with me as long as she needs," Calen said, the decision made in his heart before he spoke the words. "And no one is going to send Renee away for long. She'll get well and be on her feet again in no time. She'd want Tessie to be with me."

"I don't know," the sheriff cautioned him. "Renee could be looking at four counts of robbery. I wouldn't go making any plans right now. Besides, the family-services folks are going to ask you how you're going to take care of that little one if her mother doesn't get out for a while."

"She'll live with me," Calen repeated.

"I know that," the sheriff answered with

some irritation in his voice. "But they're going to want to know if she has a bed to sleep in and a doll to play with—that kind of thing. They're not going to be too impressed with her growing up in some bunkhouse filled with ranch hands and dirty socks."

"The men at the Elkton Ranch keep the bunkhouse neat," Calen said stiffly, as he realized he didn't know the first thing about how to take care of a little girl. He could protect her, sure. Rattlesnakes or flash floods would be no problem. But he didn't quite know what she would eat. Did she have teeth yet? He supposed she was past needing baby food.

The sheriff grunted. "Have you ever held a child in your arms?"

"I held Renee."

The sheriff gave him a look. "Recently, I mean."

"Babies are babies. They haven't changed in the past twenty years." Calen resolutely stepped closer to the car and crouched a little, holding out his arms to where Gracie sat with his granddaughter. "If you slide her out, I should be able to take her without even waking her up."

It would come back to him, Calen told himself, hoping no one noticed the sweat forming on his forehead. He saw the mothers at church picking up their toddlers all the time. No one seemed to have a problem holding one. Even the fathers managed.

Gracie had barely let go of Tessie, laying her gently in his arms, when the girl jerked awake and screamed. She turned to Gracie so quickly and with such force that Calen almost dropped her.

"I'm sorry," Calen said, as his granddaughter wrapped herself around Gracie's neck and clung to the woman as if she was her only security in this frightening storm. "My hands must be cold."

Gracie managed to give him a sympathetic glance while she began to rub Tessie on her back. "It's not that."

"Family services is not going to be impressed," the sheriff muttered as he walked a little closer, too.

Calen was feeling a touch of panic.

"Maybe she's hungry." He should have thought of that earlier. Children liked to eat. He patted his shirt pockets. Sometimes he had a piece of hard candy there.

He found nothing.

Calen looked over to ask if anyone else had candy, but what he saw left him silent. It was like looking at one of those old masterpiece paintings of the Madonna and child. Gracie was humming a tune as she soothed Tessie. The girl had a good hold on the woman's braid and had pulled it around to the front. But they were both calm, and Tessie had given up her terrified grip.

"I think—" Gracie said softly as she motioned for the sheriff to come closer. "Here—let's see if she will go to you."

Calen stepped back and watched as the sheriff confidently held out his arms to the girl. The sheriff had young daughters of his own and no doubt knew a few tricks.

No sooner had Gracie started to slide Tessie toward the sheriff than the girl started to screech even louder than before. The lawman stepped back in surprise.

"I didn't mean any harm," he sputtered. "Kids like me."

"It's not you," Gracie said confidently. "The girl is just afraid of men in general."

"But—" Calen started to protest. How was he going to take care of her if she was panic stricken around men? There were over a dozen men who lived in the bunkhouse. He might be able to get a trailer and park it near the ranch, but then who would watch Tessie while he worked? Would she learn to trust him? He suddenly realized this was all going to be more complicated than he had thought at first.

And then he saw the answer.

"She likes you," Calen said to Gracie in relief. "Maybe I could hire you to come with us and help me take care of her—just while Renee is in the hospital."

Gracie looked at him in astonishment. "Me? It's been years since I had little children around. The mothers do everything different now. Diapers are different. Baby food—I don't even know what has changed there. I think they puree their baby food now."

"Looks like you're doing fine to me," the sheriff said staunchly.

"I'll lend you a book if you need one," Tyler offered as he stepped over. "In fact, I think Angelina just got another baby book."

"But she's not due for five months," Gracie protested, at least momentarily distracted from Calen's offer.

Tyler shrugged and grinned. "She believes in preparation."

Gracie's face softened.

"So, you'll do it?" Calen pressed. He figured he better take advantage of the sentimental moment. If the woman had time to think, she'd refuse. "Ten dollars an hour sound okay?"

"I can't take your money."

"Well, I have to pay you something," Calen

insisted, feeling a little frantic. He knew that if Gracie made a deal with him, she would honor it. She never went back on her word; she'd even stayed married to Buck Stone when anyone with any sense would have left.

"I could go up to twenty dollars an hour," he offered. Now wasn't the time to look for a bargain, he told himself. He'd go to fifty if he had to, but it would only make her suspicious if he put that figure out right away.

"I really couldn't—" Gracie began.

Tyler interrupted then, with a glance at them both. "What my mother is trying to say is that you shouldn't have to pay for a favor like this. Not when you need help and we're set up to give it to you. But if you want, you could always take her to the harvest dinner at church instead to—to reciprocate, as it were. Neighborlylike."

Calen watched Gracie's mouth open and close and then open again. He figured she was as speechless as he was. Then Calen felt a slow grin spreading across his face. Tyler always did have a good head for when to throw a hook into the water.

"I'd be more than happy to take you to the harvest dinner," Calen said, crouching down so he could look inside the car and make direct eye contact with Gracie. He didn't want any misunderstanding. "I'll even get you a corsage to wear."

Gracie tried to say something, but only a squeak came out.

It sounded as though Tyler choked back a laugh, but Calen wasn't sure because the man sounded perfectly solemn when he said, "Well, it's a date then."

Gracie's face was reflected in the light from the side of the barn, and she looked a little flustered as she shot Tyler an indignant glance.

Then she cleared her throat and looked right at Calen. He remembered she had a certain regal way of holding her head when she was embarrassed, and he was seeing it now.

"We can talk about that later," she said, then pressed her lips together for a second. "First, we have to figure out whether I should keep Tessie out here at my place, or if we should take her in to see her mother now at the hospital."

As soon as Gracie took charge, Calen knew everything was going to be all right.

He stood up. "We need to take her in. It might be her only chance to see her mother for a while. I don't know how much the tyke knows about what's been happening, but I think she'll want to see her mom."

Gracie nodded. "I agree. But tomorrow, we'll call Mrs. Hargrove and ask if she can keep Tessie until we sort everything else out."

With that, Gracie swung around, preparing to get out of the car with Calen's granddaughter in her arms.

Calen didn't nod, but he didn't protest, either. He wondered what he had gotten himself into. In the various times he'd thought about going up to Gracie since she'd been back, he had never imagined anything like this. There was going to be no way he would look good in Gracie's eyes if she saw Tessie shriek every time he tried to hold her. After a while, the woman was bound to ask herself if there was something wrong with him. Maybe it would be best if Mrs. Hargrove was the one to help him after all.

Not that he had time to worry about his pride now, he told himself. They needed to go into Miles City and see how Renee was doing.

"I'll drive us there," he said.

"I don't see how you're going to do that." Gracie stood. "There's no room for a child's seat in your pickup. Not that you even have a child's seat."

Calen grimaced.

"I didn't think of that," he admitted. Then

he looked in the window of the car. "But we can use that one. It buckles right in. We'll go in—"

Calen looked around. Both Gracie and Tyler drove pickups, too.

"I'll drive all of you," the sheriff finally offered. "I'm set up to carry anyone in an emergency."

"Well, this qualifies," Calen said as he stepped close to Gracie. Tessie's eyes grew wide, but she seemed to feel safe as long as she was in Gracie's arms.

"Hold on," he said as he swept them both up together. "Let's get you to the house so you can get some shoes on. No point in anyone catching pneumonia."

Calen liked the heft of the woman and child in his arms. Tessie's face was so close he could feel her warm breath on his neck. He shifted them both slightly in his arms and thought he heard the girl giggle softly.

"You like that?" he whispered.

He regretted the question, because it made Tessie hide her face in Gracie's shoulder. It only took him a couple more steps to reach the porch, anyway.

"I'll go help the sheriff move the child seat." Calen set Gracie firmly on the bottom step to the porch. Tessie wiggled in her arms, trying to avoid looking at him.

Calen quickly dropped a kiss on the girl's head. She froze but didn't make a sound. So he kissed the top of Gracie's head, too.

He wasn't sure which of the two was more stunned.

"I'll get the door for you," Calen said then, signaling both of them that he was stepping around them.

Two steps brought him to where he could reach the knob. A twist of the hand and the door swung open.

"I won't be long," Gracie whispered, and then slipped into her house still carrying the girl.

He closed the door after they were inside. He stood on the step a moment, rubbing his cold hands. Hopefully, Gracie and Tessie would take a minute to warm up while he and the sheriff got ready to go to Miles City.

A smile split his face then. He had kissed Gracie Stone. Well, sort of.

He walked back to the sheriff.

"You got a heater in your car?" Calen asked. The man had his flashlight shining around in Renee's car still.

"Top of the line." The sheriff nodded proudly as he looked up.

"I want to be sure my girls are warm enough."

The sheriff grunted at that. "Gracie stopped being a girl some time ago."

"Not to me." Calen reached into the back of the car and unbuckled the car seat. Tyler opened the opposite door, and there was no missing the grin on his face. Gracie's son must have heard him.

"We'll have to go fishing again someday," Tyler said. "I always did enjoy sitting on the creek bed with you."

"I'll be there the first warm day we have next spring. I haven't been fishing the past year or two, and I miss it."

Tyler nodded. "I think my old fishing pole is in the barn loft."

Calen wished it was that easy to slip back into his early relationship with Gracie. Not that they'd exactly been friends in high school. She'd always been Buck Stone's girl, and he'd been a little tongue-tied around her. He glanced over at the house. Why was it that a man like him couldn't seem to get the words out of his mouth to impress a woman he cared about, when he could flirt with all of the others with ease?

He finished unbuckling the child's seat and pulled it out.

"I guess this goes in the back?" Calen asked as the lawman opened the door to the county car.

The sheriff nodded to him. "You'll sit up front with me."

"Okay." Calen figured that if he was in the front, he wouldn't have to worry about impressing Gracie with his witty conversation during the trip into Miles City.

He felt his shirt pockets again. He wished he had one of those hard mints at least. But there was nothing there. In high school, he always had wrapped candies to give to the girls. He knew that was why they came around him so often, but he'd never told Buck that. He grinned just remembering it.

He glanced over at the porch again and his grin faded. He wondered what secret Buck had that had gotten him Gracie. Calen would have traded all the hard candy in his pockets back then to know what she had seen in his friend and not in him.

Chapter Four

Gracie sat in the back of the sheriff's car and looked straight ahead. Tyler had gone home and the rest of them were headed to the hospital. It was bitter cold out, but the heat inside the vehicle was stifling, so she had removed her jacket. Now she wished she'd taken time to find a cotton blouse to go with her jeans instead of pulling on the first thing she had seen in her closet, a heavy black turtleneck. The waiting room at the hospital would be chilly, though, she reminded herself.

A few months ago, when her oldest son, Wade, had hurt his thumb, she'd dragged him there to see a doctor, and the automatic door in the reception area had seemed to open whenever anyone walked in front of it. The room got so much fresh air it was hard to heat or cool. She could still hear the incessant sliding of that door in her mind.

"Hold on," the sheriff said as he turned off the gravel road, taking a shortcut to the highway. Bits of gravel pinged against the underside of the car, but Gracie hardly noticed. The darkness was thick except for the focused beam of the county car as the sheriff drove them down the dirt road, following the path that the Elkton Ranch trucks used every fall as they took their cattle to market.

The sheriff's actions reminded Gracie of how important it was to get to the hospital quickly.

She suddenly felt apprehensive. Who knew what was happening with Renee? And it wasn't just her wound that could be giving her trouble. When Gracie had taken Wade to the clinic, the receptionist had recognized the Stone family name. Gracie wondered if Renee would face the same kind of questions from the staff that she had fielded on that day. There were not many criminals around here, and they stood out.

Gracie didn't know why people were so curious about her time in prison, but they were. Maybe it was all the cop shows that were on television. The news that she had been declared innocent had stirred up almost as much gossip as when she had been found guilty ten years ago. She frequently spoke about the Bible study group she'd belonged to in prison, but she never talked about the rest of her prison experience. She didn't want to even call up those memories. Once she started, the hopeless faces all came back to her. Susie, who had the teenage sons that refused to come to visit her. Martha, who worried about her elderly mother. The woman from Idaho who longed for the ocean and had died of an over-dose in her cell after someone had smuggled drugs in to her.

In an abrupt motion, Calen turned around to look at her, and she wondered if she had made some distressed sound without being aware of it. Just thinking about her days behind bars made her sad.

"You okay?" he asked.

She couldn't see his eyes in the dark, so she couldn't tell if they were full of pity. But then, he couldn't see her face either, so he wouldn't notice the tears that had sprung to her eyes. He probably thought the sheriff's sudden turn with the car had startled her. He should know a rancher like her knew the usefulness of all the dirt roads around here.

"Everything's fine," Gracie said, forcing herself to be cheerful, as she glanced over at the dark shape beside her. Tessie was napping in her child seat.

"I know it's late," Calen muttered apologetically, still watching her. "You must be tired."

"Don't worry about it. I wasn't sleeping anyway."

"Something worrying you?"

"Just my sons. They—" Gracie caught herself in time. Calen didn't need to know her sons were pressuring her to get married again. No one needed to know that particular fact. "They can be a little stubborn at times when they get an idea into their heads."

Calen chuckled then, his voice suddenly warm and relaxed. "What is it this time? I remember Tyler laid out his plans once for how he was going to raise a llama on your place with no one knowing. He figured he'd build a shelter for it down in the coulee where we were fishing, and feed it with oats he'd sneak away from the barn."

"I didn't know." Gracie felt exposed. How could this man know more about her youngest son than she did?

"I think it was supposed to be a Christmas surprise. Nothing ever came of it, though."

"Ahh," Gracie murmured. Her sons always had wanted a spectacular Christmas. Maybe that's why Buck had been so set against the day. Her late husband had been jealous of anything that took attention away from him. All he ever allowed in the way of a holiday celebration was to have their closest neighbors, the Mitchells, over for dinner. And, since Gracie had found out he'd been having an affair with Tilly Mitchell, she didn't suppose she could count his neighborliness as being selfless, even in that regard. Gracie had always used her best china, too, for those dinners. She shook her head at how naive she had been.

After a moment of silence, Calen turned to face the front again.

Before long, the sheriff drove the car onto the freeway. He cleared this throat almost at the same time and looked into the rearview mirror. "Did Tessie talk to you while you were in the house changing your clothes?"

"No," Gracie conceded. She wasn't sure, but she thought even a two-year-old should have a few dozen words in her vocabulary. Maybe Tessie couldn't talk normally. The toddlers at church were always chattering away.

"Well, she's been through a tough night," the lawman said.

No one had anything to add to that.

After a few more miles, Gracie noticed the extra straps on the back of the front seats. She had expected the mesh division that separated the rear seat from the driver, but she hadn't realized they'd also added new straps to these sheriff cars.

The county had gotten a new car for Sheriff Wall in the time since he had arrested her ten years ago. The vehicle still had the same smell to it, though. It wasn't unpleasant exactly, but it did make her realize that fear had an odor all its own.

Tessie wasn't the only one who had been through a lot tonight. Gracie figured the toddler's mother was only at the beginning of her ordeal. Gracie knew what it felt like to be arrested, and she figured Renee would find out before long. Everything changed once a person was on the wrong side of the law. A prison was designed to make a person feel trapped and helpless. Even though Gracie had been innocent, that did not mean the same problems that the other inmates faced didn't weigh on her mind.

"Renee's going to be worried about her daughter," Gracie said. "They probably won't let us see her yet, but one of the nurses can give Renee a message."

She wondered if that same receptionist would be on duty. If so, maybe the Stone family's notoriety could be used for something positive. If the woman took a message, Gracie might even answer one or two of her personal questions.

Gracie didn't know what would happen to Tessie if her mother went to prison, but armed robbery would carry a long sentence. She would not put that into words, but everyone in this car was probably thinking the same thing.

Gracie looked up at Calen. His shoulders were slumped a little as he sat in the front seat, his head bowed slightly. She wondered if he was praying. She hoped so. At least Renee and Tessie had him to take care of them.

And, we all have You, Father, she prayed. She hadn't had the assurance of God's love when she had gone to prison. And it would have made a huge difference.

She sat back then, trying to picture Calen as a father. Or even a husband, for that matter. She finally gave up and smiled. The stories Buck used to tell of him and Calen in high school did not match up with the man she'd seen tonight.

"Do you still have that trophy Buck gave you?" Gracie asked after a few minutes.

Calen grunted and turned around again. "That thing will be at the bottom of my closet until the day I die. Unless I sell it for junk metal first. Only Buck would give me a brass trophy that said Number One Romeo of Custer Country."

The man's voice sounded better, at least. Gracie was glad they did have some good memories they could share.

"He found that trophy in some pawnshop," Calen continued. "But he had the words re-done. I think he gave up one of his good knives in trade for it. Just to give me a hard time—calling me Romeo."

"Well, you always were popular with the girls," Gracie teased him softly.

"Not with the one that mattered," he shot back too quickly to have thought about it.

She didn't know what to say to that. She ran through the names of the girls in their class, trying to figure out which one he'd been sweet on. She was surprised Buck hadn't told her. Even though everyone knew Buck was her boyfriend, he didn't like her being around other people and she missed out on most of the gossip. For all of Calen's flirting, she couldn't remember ever hearing that he had been seri-ous about anyone.

By the time she had decided to ask him who he meant, he'd already turned around and the moment was gone. Then a semitruck passed and made too much noise for talking. She watched the red taillights for a while. There was seldom much traffic on the freeway going through this part of the state, and it was particularly deserted in the middle of the night.

Gracie settled back against the seat. She hadn't thought about those old high school days for years. The only time she had seen Calen during her marriage was that one night when he'd brought Buck home after her husband had passed out from drinking too much in some bar. She'd been so embarrassed; she'd told Calen more than she should have about her life with Buck. She couldn't bring herself to admit that her husband hit her regularly, but she knew the ranch foreman had sensed her unhappiness. She'd felt close to him that night. That's when he'd given her the number for his private phone at the Elkton bunkhouse.

Funny how she'd thought of that phone number so often back then that she'd memorized it. She'd almost dialed it a time or two when Buck had gotten particularly out of hand, but she never did. She was saving it as a last resort.

It wasn't long before Gracie saw the outlines of buildings that, even in the dark, marked the outskirts of Miles City. The hospital was at the main exit. She could tell from the green numbers on the dash of the car that it was a little after two o'clock in the morning. She hated to wake up Tessie, but they needed to be inside asking about the child's mother as soon as possible.

"They have coffee in the vending machines inside," Calen said as the sheriff pulled into the parking lot. Light streamed out of the windows of the hospital. "And I have lots of dollar bills."

Gracie nodded. The rest of the night promised to be long.

The sheriff stepped out of the car the minute it stopped and headed toward the hospital.

Soon after that, Calen closed his door, wondering if he should offer to carry Tessie. He didn't want to startle his granddaughter.

"I should have a stroller." He opened the door for Gracie so she could bring the sleeping child out of the backseat with her. "She's too heavy for—"

"For someone my age," Gracie said with a grimace as she swung her legs out of the car and then stood up, settling Tessie against her shoulder.

"She's too heavy for anyone," Calen corrected, as he moved close enough to grab Gracie if she needed help.

By that time, the sheriff was almost to the hospital.

The lawman stopped and turned. "I'll send word when I've had a chance to see Renee."

Then he stepped up to the entrance door.

"You can go with him if you want," Gracie offered as she looked over at Calen. "I know you're worried."

They were still yards from the hospital and going slow.

He shook his head. "I can't leave you alone to carry Tessie."

Calen wasn't used to someone else taking on his responsibility, even temporarily. Especially when the wind had started to blow and a few drops of cold rain had already landed on his face. Then he saw, under an overhang, just what he needed—a hospital wheelchair.

"I'll be right back," he said, as he ran over there and rolled the chair back to where Gracie stood.

"Next best thing to a stroller," Calen said. "Tessie will be fine in one of these."

Gracie looked relieved when Tessie was settled in the chair.

"I can push it," he said then. The girl was still half-asleep, but she didn't seem to care who was behind her as long as Gracie walked along beside her and held her hand. They moved much faster with the chair.

Calen blinked as they crossed through the doorway into the main waiting room of the hospital. After all the darkness of the night, the light seemed particularly bright, so they stood inside for a moment and allowed their eyes to adjust.

"You must be the father," a young woman called to Calen from the check-in desk, so he pushed the wheelchair closer.

"For Renee Hampton?" the receptionist added.

He didn't know any Hamptons, but the woman set a clipboard down on the counter in front of him.

"The paramedics said you'd be coming," she added.

"Yes." Calen felt proud. He didn't care what last name his daughter gave. He hadn't been labeled a father often in his life, and he liked the feeling.

"They said you wouldn't know much, but do your best with the forms." The woman smiled as she pointed.

Calen picked up the clipboard. "Thanks."

He noticed then that the woman's smile tightened. She'd finally noticed Gracie standing beside him. "You're Mrs. Stone, aren't you?"

The receptionist's voice was barely polite. It had an avid tone to it, though, as if she expected something awful to happen and was anticipating it.

Gracie didn't respond in kind. She nodded and smiled quite pleasantly. "I was hoping you can tell us how Renee is doing."

"I'm afraid that would be a violation of our policy," the receptionist said, more shortly than was necessary, in Calen's opinion.

"Did Sheriff Wall go in?" Calen asked, thinking maybe that was the reason for the sudden coldness.

The receptionist nodded. Her eyes warmed as she looked at him. "But he didn't say why."

"Good," Gracie muttered at his side. "Shows some sense."

The receptionist did not even look at Gracie.

Calen thought the awkwardness might be in his own mind until the young woman leaned forward, speaking to the side as though to shut Gracie out. "One of the paramedics told me Renee had been shot. And not in a hunting accident, if you know what I mean."

"That's nothing but speculation," Gracie responded sharply, and then stepped closer to the counter as though forcing the young woman to deal with her.

The hospital worker, her cheeks bright pink from the reproof, did not respond.

"I'm sure the sheriff will sort it all out." Calen kept his voice as neutral as possible. Years of managing squabbles among the men on the Elkton Ranch had taught him not to throw fuel on any fire. There were no other people in the waiting room, but a public spectacle would do no good right now.

Calen turned then and, motioning for Gracie to go first, started to push the wheelchair over to a line of chairs on the opposite wall. A stack of blankets sat on a small table next to the chairs. He figured Gracie only accompanied him because he had Tessie. The woman was still upset.

Calen picked a pink blanket from the stack and spread it over his granddaughter. Then he sat down.

"People shouldn't gossip," Gracie whispered after she lowered herself into the chair next to him.

"There's no way we can keep something like this quiet." Calen looked over at Gracie. In the light, he could see that her hair was partially pulled out of her braid. Tessie's work, no doubt. He felt the urge to smooth the hair back, but he didn't think she would like it.

"The newspapers around here are pretty good, though," he finally said. "They know not to speculate too much, especially if there's going to be a trial."

"That's not the way I remember it," Gracie protested, her voice low and bitter. "The newspapers around here print anything if they think it will sell a few more papers. They certainly covered my return last year. Like the arrest itself a decade ago wasn't enough."

Calen crossed his leg so he could rest the clipboard on his right foot, but he didn't start filling in the information. He cleared his throat instead and said the words he owed her. "I should have apologized years ago for not coming to your defense when you were arrested."

"I never asked for any help."

He nodded. "That doesn't mean I shouldn't have offered it."

Gracie didn't say anything. She stared down at the floor as if she was caught up in memories.

"I was baking a cake that day," she finally said as she looked up. "A lemon chiffon. Buck's favorite. We'd had a fight about letting the boys go ice skating. I thought maybe if he had a piece of cake, he'd change his mind. It was a few days after Christmas, and I thought they needed to have some fun before they went back to school. It wasn't until I heard Wade yelling from the barn that I knew something was wrong."

Calen reached over and took Gracie's hand. She was shaking with emotion.

"I never did ask the boys what they did with that cake," she continued. "The sheriff arrested me in the barn the minute I told him I'd done it. He never even let me go into the house to take the cake out of the oven. Or get a jacket. Or say goodbye to my boys."

Suddenly, holding Gracie's hand wasn't enough. He put his arm around her and drew her close to him. "It's all right now."

She shook her head. "It's not about me. I just want Renee to know how fast things change. One day you're baking a cake and the next—" Gracie stopped to swallow. "Nothing is ever the same after that. This time in the hospital. It might be the only free time she has with her daughter."

Gracie didn't move away from him and he left his arm where it was. They sat that way for a good twenty minutes, and then Sheriff Wall came back into the waiting room.

"How is she?" Calen asked when the man was close enough to hear him.

"Doing pretty good," the lawman said as he walked over to them.

If the sheriff noticed Calen's arm around Gracie, he didn't say anything.

"When can we see her?" Gracie asked.

"Not until morning," the sheriff said. "The doctors shooed me out. They need to clean out her wound and stitch it up. The anesthesia will put her out for the rest of the night."

"What happens then?" Calen asked.

"Just as soon as she wakes up and is coherent, I'm going to take what statement she's willing to give. All she's asked about so far, besides Tessie, was whether or not we have that man she calls her husband. Denny Hampton. They have him in the jail up in Havre. I don't see why she's so worried about him. He's worthless, in my opinion. He ran off after the robbery and left her to fend for herself."

"She wants to know if he's coming after her," Gracie said as she leaned forward till she was no longer touching Calen's arm. "Husband or not, he's likely the one beating up on her."

Calen figured he could take a hint. He casually moved his arm so it was no longer behind her. She seemed more at ease then.

The sheriff nodded to Gracie. "Makes sense. She said there's another man, too—a Carter Benson. Said he left them two days ago to head back to Michigan where he grew up."

"So it didn't have to be Renee in those holdups?" Calen asked, hope in his voice. It was time for some good news.

The sheriff shrugged. "I wouldn't say that.

We have enough to question her in the latest one. We'll have to wait and see about the others."

They were all silent for a moment.

"We don't have any record of this Carter fellow." The sheriff shifted his stance. "He might not even exist. Criminals often say someone else did it. It's the oldest lie in the book."

Gracie drew in a sharp breath. "Sometimes it *was* someone else who did it, though."

The sheriff had the grace to blush, but he also seemed a little indignant. "I had no idea you weren't telling me the honest truth that day in the barn. You just walked up and confessed. What was I to think?"

"I know that," Gracie countered, and then stopped to draw a breath.

Calen figured he better do something before the situation got out of hand. He looked down at the hospital form. "Did anyone notice if Renee had any cigarettes on her? I don't even know if she smokes. They have a whole line of questions about Renee's health history."

The sheriff and Gracie both shook their heads.

It wasn't much of a distraction, but it seemed to get them past the tense conversation.

"I'm going to check with the jail in Havre," the lawman announced after a moment. "See if Denny Hampton knows anything about this other guy."

"That would be helpful," Gracie said, clearly trying to be polite.

"Denny hasn't been talking, so it's a long shot," the sheriff warned them before he turned to leave.

Gracie was silent as she watched the lawman walk out of the waiting room. Over by the reception area, the young woman they had talked to was speaking animatedly with two other staff members.

"The sheriff could always ask those women," Gracie said, nodding her head toward the three hospital workers. "The grapevine around this place seems to always know everything about local criminals."

"They're just kids," Calen said softly. "I suppose they think it's exciting. They don't mean any harm."

"And yet they cause it," Gracie said, pressing her lips together.

She sat silent for a few minutes, even after the receptionist sat down at her desk and the two other staff members left the area.

"You don't need to stay," Calen offered. "I

can handle Tessie now that I have the wheel-chair."

Gracie looked over at him. Her dark eyes were troubled and, if he wasn't mistaken, she was on the verge of tears. "I should leave. That would be best for you."

"I'm not worried about what is best for me," Calen retorted. "I just don't like to see you put yourself through this."

Gracie winced. "It doesn't do you any good to have me here. Those staff members you see are asking questions, trying to figure out why I'm here to see about Renee and what happened. By now, they're probably wondering if she and I knew each other in prison. If maybe we were cell mates. If somehow the plan, all along, was for her to lay low at my place after the robberies."

"That's nonsense," Calen protested. "Surely people aren't—"

He stopped when he saw a woman in a business suit come over to the receptionist's desk. She looked like a manager and was frowning as she scolded the young woman for something. Maybe Gracie wasn't too far off with her suspicions.

"I'm sorry," he said. "Sometimes people are truly thoughtless."

Gracie didn't answer.

"Mrs. Hargrove gets up at six," Gracie finally said. "You can call her by seven to ask for her help. I bet Tessie talks up a storm when she's with her."

Calen tried to smile. "You might feel different in the morning. Tessie likes you."

"She's special, isn't she?"

"You're our first choice."

Gracie smiled and nodded. "I'm glad to help then. Just let me get some sleep. I'm tired."

Calen wasn't sure of himself, but he knew he had to do it anyway. He moved closer to Gracie and put his arm around her again. This time he wasn't helping her with Tessie. This was just for him and her.

"I've got you," he said and felt her relax. "You don't need to worry. I'll watch out for everything while you close your eyes and rest."

She leaned into him after that, nestling under his arm. He reached up and smoothed back the hair that Tessie had managed to pull out of her braid.

"I finally called that number you gave me all those years ago," Gracie murmured, her eyes smiling at him.

"I'm glad you did."

Calen figured there was no need to tell her that he'd paid extra to keep that number over the years. He'd switched rooms several times in the bunkhouse and had paid to have a phone installed each time so he could take the number with him. He'd even spent money to keep the number reserved for him when he'd moved away from Dry Creek for those few years.

An orderly pushed a cart past the entrance of the waiting room and the doors opened, letting in a cold draft. Calen looked down and saw that Tessie was still sleeping, slumped to the side in the wheelchair with her blanket covering her.

"We should all get some rest." Calen reached to the side and took another one of the blankets, this one beige. He draped it over Gracie's shoulders and tucked it between them, in the place under his arm where she was pressed against him. She closed her eyes as though she was weary.

Then he leaned over and kissed her forehead.

"What's that for?" she muttered sleepily.

He smiled. "Nothing."

"You always were a Romeo," she whispered without opening her eyes. "A woman in every port, Buck used to say."

"I never did take to the sea," he corrected her mildly, but she was already falling asleep. He wondered suddenly how different their futures would have been if he'd been the first one to ask Gracie out on a date in high school. He had wanted to, but his nerves had failed him. By the time he got the courage back, Buck had asked her instead.

He closed his eyes. Maybe there was time yet to find out where the feelings he had for her would lead if he let them. And then the realization hit him with the force of a sledge-hammer, and his eyes flew open. What was he thinking? He couldn't court Gracie. Not now. She was right. Gossip would start up again about her if she was friendly with him and his family. People might not know Renee's maiden name right now, but they would find it out. She was involved in those robberies in some way, and she was his daughter. Gracie would suffer her worst nightmare all over again if she tried to stand by him. And, this time, it would be his fault for letting her.

Chapter Five

Gracie woke with a start. Something was rattling around and she glanced over at the clock on the wall. It was six-thirty in the morning and a man dressed in white was pushing a cart across the front of the waiting room, the wheels making that sound as they rolled on the tile floor. Gracie shrugged off the blanket that had covered her shoulders and yawned, taking a deep breath as she stretched. The smell of bacon was mingling with the antiseptic odor of the hospital, so she figured the cart held breakfast for the patients. She could do with something to eat herself.

The cart disappeared around a corner and the sunlight coming into the room from the glass windows seemed to get stronger. Slender tree branches brushed against the windows, showing there was a breeze outside. The cold weather had stripped leaves off all the trees and left them bare already this year.

"Good morning."

The raspy voice startled Gracie and she turned to see Calen walking toward her, gingerly holding two cups in his hands. His shirt was rumpled and his hair needed to be patted down. As he stepped close, he held out a cup. "Coffee?"

"Thank you." Gracie took what he offered and brought it to her lips so she could take her first sip. "Ahhh. It's perfect."

"Good." Calen sat down with his own cup.

Gracie took another long sip and then frowned. The coffee was too perfect. She looked over at the man. "How did you know I take cream and no sugar?"

"Church," Calen said easily.

"You've been watching me in church?" Gracie knew she shouldn't keep frowning, but she couldn't seem to help it.

Calen shrugged. "It's not a crime to notice things."

"Well, no, but—"

"You know, they don't have anything in those vending machines that's worth eating for breakfast," Calen said, sounding disgusted. "I could have bought you a chocolate bar with almonds or a supersize pack of chewing gum. Now, I ask you, is that any kind of a balanced meal?"

Gracie took another gulp and felt the warmth of the beverage slide down her throat.

"Just the coffee is enough," she said after she had finished swallowing. She supposed she couldn't sue a man for watching her—which made her wonder what her hair looked like. She glanced sideways to see if Calen was noticing her now, but he seemed caught up in his thoughts. Which was good. Her braid had unraveled last night, so her hair was probably so tangled that she resembled that Medusa creature. The Greek one. Gracie always carried a comb in her purse, but she hadn't brought her purse with her last night. Instead she'd had Tessie in her arms.

She smiled slightly as she looked down at the girl. The little one's face was pink in the morning light, except for a deep red crease that showed where she'd lain against the back bar of the wheelchair all night.

"I hate to wake her," Gracie said as she turned to Calen, wondering how she'd grown so fond of this little girl in such a short time. She was glad she was going to be taking care of her. "But I should at least wash her face in case they let us in to see her mother."

"Ah," Calen said, and dropped his gaze to the floor. "About that—"

She knew there was nothing on the tile of any interest, so she figured he was looking there so he wouldn't have to look at her.

"Renee is still here, isn't she?" Gracie asked in alarm. "They didn't take her to a jail somewhere or anything?"

Things could have changed in the years since Gracie had been arrested.

"No, no," Calen looked up and assured her quickly. "I think they'll let us talk to her pretty soon. After the sheriff finishes what he needs to do."

"Oh, that's—" Gracie stopped. She'd started to say it was good, but it was clearly not that good. "It's okay. I guess that's the best we can expect."

Maybe Calen was just tired, she told herself when he still didn't so much as glance at her.

He took a long drink of coffee and sat silently for another few minutes. "I've decided I'm going to call Mrs. Hargrove after all. See if she can take over with Tessie."

"Take over?" If he'd said that last night, she would have been fine with it. But now that she'd had some sleep, she felt more hopeful about everything. She didn't want to let Tessie go. Not that it was her decision to make.

"It makes sense, of course," Gracie said, trying not to feel bad about it. "Mrs. Hargrove is better with children than I am."

"That's not true. You're great."

"And tomorrow is Sunday," Gracie added, reminding herself of everything as she spoke. "Mrs. Hargrove probably wants to spend part of today preparing for her Sunday-school class, but it will do Tessie good to go and be with the other kids."

"You could do just as good of a job as she does," Calen said, and then stopped to turn to her. "Mrs. Hargrove prepares her lesson?"

"You would know that if you had *observed* her," Gracie said with a bite to her words that she hadn't planned to show. "Or do you only look at people during the coffee time?"

Calen flushed. "I do know she takes honey in her tea."

Gracie nodded and tried to pull back from her emotions. It was his family; his call. "That she does."

"But the kids—it's not like these are junior-high kids," he persisted. "She teaches the toddlers and kindergarten class. What does she need to prepare? They aren't going to ask any hard questions."

Gracie thought he must be feeling as testy as she was or he would have let it go already.

It had been a hard night. A good fight would clear the tension between them, but it was no fun when they both knew the argument was not real.

She grinned. "I don't think it's the questions. I think she spends most of her preparation time in prayer."

"Oh."

That put him in his place, but she didn't feel good about it.

"Don't worry. She'll know what to do for Tessie," Gracie added as a peace offering. Tessie was the important thing. "I don't know how she does it, but Mrs. Hargove has a gift. She could coax a blind man to see. A deaf man to hear. A—" Gracie broke off and looked over at Calen. "You do think Tessie *can* talk, don't you? I know she's shy. And last night had to be frightening for her. That has to be it, don't you think?"

Calen took another sip of coffee. She realized it was probably to give himself more time to form his words.

"I've never known a Gray yet who couldn't talk," he finally said, his voice just a shade too hearty to be convincing. "I expect Tessie will get comfortable with us before long and we won't be able to stop her flow of words."

Calen looked as though he was trying to

smile, and failing. Finally, he gave it up, sitting there with an expression on his face that was so glum Gracie regretted even posing the question. She reached over and patted his hand. "Don't listen to me. Like I said, I don't know anything about kids these days. Besides, even if she can't talk, it's probably just a temporary thing. They have people now who help children with that kind of a problem."

"I could pay someone," Calen agreed, looking relieved.

"Mrs. Hargrove will know what to do," Gracie assured him.

Since that was the truth of it, Gracie sat there feeling a little useless. She knew it was foolish to wish she could still be the one to take care of the girl. She'd had the joy of raising three boys and that was enough for the heart of any woman. And, truly, she didn't have enough time to read the books Tyler and Angelina had at their house. She didn't have nine months to prepare for a troubled child. She didn't know anything about cartoons or the dolls she heard the mothers at church talking about.

Leaning down to pat Tessie on the head, Gracie consoled herself with the thought that she could make a difference by praying for the child. That would be her part in taking care of her.

When Gracie looked back up, she saw that Calen was squinting at something beyond the main window.

"Isn't that Charley Nelson?" he finally muttered as he pointed.

Gracie looked. A man was walking in from the parking lot, his hand clamped down on the gray Stetson on his head, obviously trying to keep it from blowing away. The man's build looked like Charley's, all right.

"What would he be doing here at this hour?" Gracie asked as she tried to see the man more clearly. Her sons had told her she needed new glasses and maybe they were right. With his head down, the man was hard to identify. "That brown jacket looks like Charley's. They don't make plaid wool ones like that anymore."

"We can be thankful for that," Calen said. "They smell worse than summer sheep if you get them wet in the rain. Can you see if there's an oil stain on the front corner of the jacket?"

"Of course not." Gracie looked further out into the parking lot. "And I don't see Mrs. Hargrove, either. They would both be here, wouldn't they?"

"They always go everywhere together,"

Calen agreed, and then shook his head as though he disapproved. "They are the poster couple for wedded bliss round here. All peace and harmony."

Gracie stared at him. "Do you have something against marriage?"

"No." Calen straightened in his chair. "Nothing at all."

"Good, because—"

"Just jealous I suppose," he said, before she could make her point.

When he said that, Gracie couldn't even remember what she had been going to say. They had no need to bicker anyway. She did hope, though, that she hadn't looked that sour when she'd told her sons she wasn't interested in marriage. She turned her gaze back to the window. She really should try to keep an open mind on the subject.

The man who was walking toward the door was making slow progress, hunched as he was against the wind. A quality man like Charley Nelson, if he was younger by three decades and still single, would be a good choice for a husband, she told herself, feeling vindicated that she wasn't set against marriage itself. She had just not found the right man.

"How long have they been married now?"

she asked, turning to Calen. "Mrs. Hargrove and Charley."

Their whole courtship had happened while she was away, and she regretted not having been in Dry Creek to see it. She might have picked up some tips.

"Four years," Calen said then. "Or is it five now?"

The man finally reached the building and stepped close enough for the sliding glass door to open, allowing him to enter. When he had, he looked up and removed his hat, which meant Gracie could see him.

"Charley," Gracie called in delight and stood up to wave. Then she turned to her companion. "You were right."

Calen nodded, clearly pleased with himself. "The guys out at the ranch have been telling me I need glasses, but I've still got good eyes."

Gracie started to walk toward the door, scanning the distant parking lot behind Charley as she went. Her eyes might not be as good as they had been when she was younger, but she could not find a gray-haired woman wandering around out there. Mrs. Hargrove must be in the car.

"I just can't believe the nerve of some people." Charley started to complain before he even got close enough so that she could greet him properly.

"You've heard, then?" Gracie felt relieved. She should have known Mrs. Hargrove would come to her rescue, even if she had to use her husband to do so.

"I came in to get Edith's blood pressure pills," Charley continued, sounding as though he had not even heard what she had said. "Those clerks at the counter always give me a hard time when I pick up her medications because we don't have the same last name."

Okay, Gracie realized. Charley didn't have a clue about what had happened. She glanced over at the reception desk and noticed a new staff person was sitting there.

"I wasn't opposed when Edith wanted to keep her old name when we got married," Charley said, almost muttering to himself. "She was worried that the Sunday-school class children would have a hard time remembering a new name if she had one. So I was okay with it. You don't want to go against Edith and the children."

He paused and finally looked up at Gracie.

"I always say it isn't the name, but the affection in the heart that is important anyway," he explained to her. "But the people in the pharmacies just don't see it that way."

Gracie nodded. "Well, everybody knows you're married."

"Knowing isn't enough anymore. They want proof." Charley shook his head until gradually a twinkle appeared in his eyes. "It won't do Edith's blood pressure any good when I tell her the pharmacy thinks we're living together without benefit of a license, either. I can tell you that much."

Gracie chuckled. "You're right on that."

They had stopped midway across the room and, after a bit, Charley started to look over at the chairs. "Isn't that Calen Gray? What's he doing here?"

Charley didn't give her time to answer. He started to walk over. "Hey, Calen. What's happening? One of the Elkton men come down sick?"

"The men are all fine," Calen said.

"Glad to hear it." Charley nodded and then turned to Gracie. "But you're the one I'm so glad to see here. Edith needs your help. She's probably called your house already and left a message."

"What's wrong?" Gracie asked. She was glad she'd finally been asked for something. Edith had done so much for her over the years.

"She needs someone to take over her Sunday-school class for tomorrow and was hoping you would do it."

"Me?" Gracie asked. There had to be some misunderstanding.

Charley nodded. "She said you wouldn't want to do it, but she really needs your help on this one. There's no one else."

"There has to be someone else," Gracie said, finally taking a deep breath. "Doesn't Doris June usually teach the class if her mother can't?"

Doris June Nelson was Mrs. Hargrove's daughter. She had inherited her mother's love for things like teaching Sunday school, and a more responsible person couldn't be found anywhere. Gracie told herself the spiritual welfare of the Dry Creek children should be in the hands of someone like that.

Charley shrugged. "Doris June has the flu."

"Well, then, Mrs. Redfern." Gracie felt sure that the young mothers would be comfortable leaving their children with the rancher's wife.

"Flu," Charley said.

"Glory, the pastor's wife?"

"Flu."

Gracie was beginning to feel a little desperate. "Does Mrs. Hargrove have the flu, too?"

Charley nodded.

"Well, everybody can't have the flu," she

finally said, as she looked around the waiting room. Now that Charley mentioned it, there were a lot more people in the room than there had been ten minutes ago. Even the heavy coats most of them were wearing didn't hide the fact that they had come in their pajamas and had a pasty-white look on their faces.

"Everybody doesn't have the flu," Charley finally announced triumphantly. Gracie's heart soared. "You're looking healthy."

"Well, don't look at me. It takes more than good health to teach that Sunday-school class," Gracie protested. "Those kids are impressionable."

"You'll do fine," Charley said.

Gracie was struck dumb. She didn't know how to point out that there would be a petition circulating if she attempted to teach Sunday school. "The mothers won't accept me."

There, Gracie thought. She'd said it.

Charley frowned as though he hadn't heard her. And Calen was looking at her as if she'd announced she was a space alien.

"Of course, they accept you," Calen finally said into the silence. "You've lived here for years. Well, except for—" He stopped then. "But you're innocent."

She looked at him, wondering if all men were so slow.

"The mothers might worry that I'll forget and say something that's too harsh or too scary or just plain heathen and be a bad example for their children," Gracie said, trying to explain.

Tessie gurgled and Gracie looked down. She wondered how Calen could be so clueless.

Then again, maybe he wasn't. "You don't even want me to take care of Tessie. And her life hasn't been any picnic. I doubt I could talk about anything that she hasn't already seen."

"That's not why—" Calen started to protest.

"Don't worry about that now," Charley said, an odd, pained look washing over his face. He looked as if he was starting to sweat. Then he pinned Gracie with his eyes. "Edith wouldn't ask you to take over if she thought you couldn't do it."

I—" Gracie opened her mouth and tried to say it was impossible, but she couldn't. Mrs. Hargrove was the one person in Dry Creek who had written to her when she was in prison. Gracie would crawl over hot coals on her hands and knees for that woman. But teach her Sunday-school class?

"I don't feel so good," Charley said then, his face growing whiter by the minute. "I think I'd better go home."

With that, the older man turned and started stumbling back to the door.

"Wait, Charley," Calen called after the man.

Gracie sat down in the chair next to the wheelchair.

"You understand, don't you, Tessie?" she said as the little blonde girl looked up at her with her innocent blue eyes.

Tessie didn't say anything, but she did wrinkle up her nose and put her hand in her mouth so she could start chewing on it. If Gracie wasn't mistaken, the look the toddler gave her was a little accusatory.

"I guess we've all got our troubles, don't we?" Gracie said, and started looking around. There had to be someplace to buy the child a piece of toast or something for breakfast. After all, it was going to be a long day. And Tessie was right. They deserved something to eat.

It took Calen five minutes to get the older man a temporary bed in the walk-in part of the hospital, and fifteen minutes for the men at the Elkton Ranch to draw straws to see who would drive into Miles City and escort Charley back to Dry Creek.

"I'd take you home myself," he said to the

older man as he turned to leave him in the curtained-off area. "But I need to see about Renee."

Charley lifted his head off the pillow at that. "Your daughter, Renee? The detectives finally found her? Why didn't you tell me?"

"She found me," Calen said, and then tried to loosen the elastic on the germ mask he wore. "I'll tell you all about it later. You just get some rest. The staff will let you know when someone from the ranch is here to pick you up."

"I don't want to make anyone else sick," Charley mumbled as he lay back down.

"The nurse promised to give whoever comes to get you a mask." Almost everyone in the waiting room wore one of the masks over their mouth by now. Calen had only put one on because he didn't want to give the doctors any reason that he couldn't see Renee when the sheriff was finished with her.

"Edith will want to have you and Renee over for dinner," Charley said, his voice weak by then.

"We'll talk about it later." Calen swept the curtain aside so he could pass.

Calen was glad to see that Gracie had put masks on herself and Tessie and moved the wheelchair as far back in the corner as possible. Tessie was sitting on her lap.

"I wish I had my pickup here," Calen said as he walked closer to them. "At least we could go out and sit in it, away from all these sick people here in the waiting room."

"No time for that," Gracie said as she stood up, lifting Tessie to her hip as she went. "Sheriff Wall came out and said we can go back and see Renee any time now."

Calen braced himself. "Did the sheriff say what the status was?"

Gracie nodded. "Her wound is healing nicely."

"That's not what I meant."

"She'll be transferred to jail," Gracie said, her voice crisp. "She confessed to being involved. The sheriff read her rights to her and completed the arrest."

The lack of pity in Gracie's voice steadied Calen. "We don't want to waste any time then."

"She might get out on bail," Gracie said, leaving Tessie's wheelchair behind as they went. "There's hope."

Calen nodded. He was suddenly realizing that his daughter had come to him when she needed help. He might wish she had come a few years sooner, but she had known he'd do whatever he could to help her, and that made him feel good.

It did not take long for them to arrive at the door of Renee's room.

"Oh." Calen hadn't expected to see a fully armed deputy sheriff sitting on a chair just outside the room.

"It's protocol," Gracie said as she noticed his surprise. "Don't mention it to Renee, though. If anyone overhears, they might think you're trying to warn her. Or give her information for an escape. Or who knows what."

Calen looked sideways at Gracie. He finally understood what she had been saying earlier. She did know things the other women at church didn't. He had always thought she just liked to keep to herself during the coffee time at church, but maybe there was more to it than that. Maybe the women really didn't welcome her.

It made him want to give her a hug, but he wasn't sure she'd appreciate it right now. It was unlike him to be so emotional, anyway. He hoped he wasn't coming down with something. So, instead, he stopped just outside the door and turned to her. "I'm glad you're here."

Gracie's face looked a little rosy after that, and she didn't look at him. But she did make eye contact with the guard.

At the man's nod, she pushed the door to Renee's room open.

Father, we need You, Calen prayed as he followed Gracie. *For so many things.*

Chapter Six

Gracie tightened her hold on Tessie as she stepped into the hospital room. The bed closest to the window was the only one that had anyone lying in it. A blue-and-white-striped privacy curtain was partially drawn so Gracie could not see Renee. At the bottom of the bed there was a long shape that had to be the young woman's legs.

Calen followed closely behind Gracie and, when she paused after entering the room, he reached out to touch her on the arm. She glanced over her shoulder at him.

Lord, be with us, Gracie prayed silently. She could see the turmoil on Calen's face as he looked from her to the daughter he hadn't spoken to in years and then back again.

Gracie smiled at him with encouragement.

He nodded and stepped closer. "Renee."

"Daddy?" the weary voice came from behind the curtain.

Gracie stayed back to give Calen a moment with his daughter before showing Tessie that her mother was on the other side of the curtain. Gracie pulled a tissue from the box beside the bed and gave it to the girl so she'd have something to play with. The low murmur of voices reached Gracie's ear, and she sat down on the unoccupied bed, settling Tessie on her lap. Calen and his daughter had much to talk about, and Tessie seemed content to shred the tissue.

Before long, however, the tissue was in tiny pieces and Tessie was pulling at the blue mask around her face. Gracie adjusted the elastic so that it fit looser around the girl's ears.

Within minutes, Calen stepped back from the bed and Renee called for Tessie.

Gracie carried the girl over to the bed and set her down.

"Mommy," Tessie said, proving that she could talk if she chose.

Gracie stepped away once Tessie was securely positioned on her mother's bed. Then she motioned for Calen to join the family circle in her place.

Times like these were important for a family, Gracie told herself as she walked back to the other bed. She was grateful to Sheriff Wall for allowing it. She would have given anything to be able to talk to her sons right after the lawman had arrested her all those years ago. Not that a mother could ever prepare her children for the long separation that was ahead, but she could have at least assured them of her love.

Sunshine warmed the room as Gracie sat on the edge of the bed, trying to listen to the cadence of the conversation. She'd listened like that in her own home years ago, searching for any undercurrents of anger that meant an outburst was about to come. She thought she had gotten pretty good at sensing an oncoming outburst and was relieved that Renee sounded as if she was in control of herself.

Twenty minutes later Sheriff Wall stepped back into the room.

"Is it time?" she asked him quietly.

He nodded. "We have transport for her. There is an infirmary in the jail and it will be easier to guard her there. We can put her on a twenty-four-hour lockdown if needed to keep her away from others."

"Surely, no one thinks she's going to walk out of the place," Gracie said, her tone stronger than she realized until the words left her mouth. She looked up at the sheriff. "I'm sorry. I know you've done your best here. Letting her talk to Calen and Tessie was kind."

The sheriff's lips tightened. "I'm sorry I didn't do as well for you. I had no need to rush you all those years ago. It was my first murder, though, and I was green. I wasn't sure how to handle it."

Gracie reached over and touched his arm. "I think we were all in shock. Things like that don't happen in Dry Creek. At least they hadn't until then."

The lawman nodded. "This with Renee is different, though. The rush to get her out of here isn't because we're worried she'll try something. It's because of that Carter Benson that she mentioned. It's not his real name, of course, but we've established there were definitely two men in the first robberies. Whoever the man is, he's still loose and she's the only one who can ID him, except for that husband of hers, and he's not talking. If Benson knows Renee was shot, he might know she's here."

"Oh," Gracie said, frowning. "She's in danger?"

"I'm not sure, but we want to keep her safe," the sheriff said. "The whole countryside is in and out of the hospital today, with all the flu. A stranger could easily get around here, and no one would know. Especially with those masks everyone is wearing."

Gracie nodded.

"But that's good news, isn't it?" Gracie finally said. "That she was only in on the last robbery?"

The sheriff shrugged. "We'll have to see what we can piece together. I have a suspicion she was right when she said her husband forced her to do the last robbery with him, but we can't prove anything one way or the other until he talks. And he isn't doing that."

"She has those bruises. They should count for something."

"We're going to try and get a better report of the actions during the robbery from the man they tried to rob. The one who shot her. He just gave a brief statement earlier."

Just then, two orderlies stepped inside the room, one of them pulling a gurney.

"Your ride's here, Renee," the sheriff said, loud enough to be heard on the other side of the curtain.

One of the orderlies walked over and pulled back the curtain. After that, Renee kissed Tessie's face, and Gracie walked over to pick the girl up.

Gracie expected Tessie to struggle at being removed from her mother, but she seemed resigned. The poor thing was obviously used to disappointment of every kind at her young age.

"You'll take care of her for me, won't you?" Renee looked up and asked Gracie.

The bruises on the woman had yellowed in the night, and there were dark circles around her eyes. Her face was fine boned; her violet eyes filled with vulnerability. Even with the discoloration, she was beautiful.

Gracie nodded, holding the toddler. "I'll do everything I can."

"She's a good girl," Renee added, glancing at her daughter and blinking back tears. "She's a little afraid of men, but that's all."

"I know." Gracie wondered if that was really the only thing that frightened Tessie, given how little she fussed when she was in her arms. If Tessie was a sensitive child, she had seen too much violence in her short life so far.

"Time to go," the sheriff repeated as the orderlies stepped into position next to the gurney.

Gracie stepped closer to Calen. Together they stood and watched as Renee was lifted from the bed and put on the gurney. Then, without any more words, the orderlies pushed the conveyance out to the hall, and the sheriff followed.

Inside the room, they were silent for a few minutes.

"Renee probably has things in her car that she needs," Gracie finally muttered to Calen, as they both looked at the empty doorway almost as if they thought the gurney might come back. "I think they'll let her have some personal items. A comb. Lipstick. Clothes to wear if she goes before a judge. Maybe a book to read."

Calen nodded. "I had so much I wanted to ask her."

Then he looked at Gracie. "How do I catch up in fifteen minutes when she's been gone for years? I don't even know what kind of books she reads. Or if she reads."

"You just do the best you can," Gracie said as she adjusted Tessie's mask again.

Sheriff Wall came back into the room then. "The deputies will handle it from here. I can take you home if you want."

"We'd appreciate that," Calen said, putting his arm around Gracie.

She didn't protest. She knew it wasn't only her he was embracing. It was as close as Calen could come to hugging his granddaughter and, at a time like this, he needed all the comfort he could get. She shifted the girl so Tessie was in the arm closest to Calen.

"I'll fix us some breakfast when we get to my place," Gracie offered, as she noticed Tessie didn't freeze up this time. She stared at her grandfather, but didn't tremble.

"What would you like to eat?" she asked, continuing to look down at the girl.

Tessie looked back up at her for a long minute. Then she said, her young voice clear, "Cracker."

"Well." Gracie felt like she'd been honored. "She spoke to us."

"We're going to be all right," Calen added with determination in his voice.

Gracie believed him as they all started walking out of the room together. She'd never quite realized before what a force Calen was. She should have known, if for no other reason than that he commanded the group of cowboys at the Elkton Ranch with such ease. Still, it made her glad to know that he was not giving up on his daughter and granddaughter.

An hour later, Calen sat down in Gracie's kitchen. Someone had added a coat of light green paint to the walls since the Stones had come back, and there were new white curtains on the windows. Tessie sat in a high chair that

Gracie had brought out from a back room. Surprisingly enough, it was only a little after nine o'clock in the morning, even though it felt as though a whole day had passed.

"You still have the same table," Calen said as he lightly ran his hand over the oak wood. He could feel with his fingers the ribbed scars from the years of use. Many a wet glass had sat on the surface. In fact, he'd set some of them there himself as a boy.

"Oh, that old thing has been in the Stone family for over a hundred years," Gracie said, as she brought a plate of fried eggs to the table. She'd already set down a plate of wheat pancakes and two cups of coffee. "I had the piece refinished, but I can't replace it. The boys would never let me."

Gracie went over to the high chair and straightened the bib that Tessie was wearing. The girl had a graham cracker in one hand and was watching Calen suspiciously as she chewed on it.

He winked at his granddaughter and she ducked her head.

"She's shy," Gracie said fondly, as she put her hand on the girl's head.

"I know," Calen said, looking away so Tessie could eat her cracker in peace. She wasn't the first shy child to sit here, either.

"It's a fine table." Calen remembered that he'd been a little intimidated when he'd first sat here as a boy. His mother had been a widow and needed to work so she had brought him over for Mrs. Stone to babysit. He must have been three years old at the time. "Buck and I used to eat our sandwiches here when we were kids. Did he ever mention that?"

Calen ran his hand along the underside of the wood. The two of them had carved a galloping horse there one afternoon. It was the day he knew Buck was his friend.

Gracie shook her head as she sat down. "He wasn't much for talking about the past."

"I found it," Calen exclaimed, his hand still under the table. Then he looked at a bewildered Gracie. "Just something Buck and I did after I'd been here a few years. It's a stallion. Carved with the sharpest pocketknives we had. We must have been six years old."

"I'm surprised your mothers let you have any knives at that age."

"They didn't know." Calen pulled his hand back. "And the knives weren't much sharper than putty knives, so we scratched more than cut, but we thought we were grown-up. Of course, we had the sense to carve it on the underside and not the top. We weren't that young and foolish."

Gracie smiled then. "That sounds like Buck. And he might not have said much, but he was proud of this place, so if he let you put your mark on this table with him, that said something about his feelings for you. All of those ancestors of his, all living on this land. It was everything to him."

Calen nodded. He knew that to be true. As a boy, he had liked spending time in this house, and it wasn't all because of Buck. The place was full of life. He'd hated to see it go downhill while it stood empty after Gracie had gone away.

He looked up in time to see the satisfied look Gracie had on her face as she surveyed the table, too. "I've always tried to be grateful when my family sits down here to eat. Not all children have this kind of a legacy. Buck's great-grandparents built this ranch when there was nothing around but wild prairie grass and rattlesnakes."

They were both silent for a moment.

"But how about you?" Calen finally asked. "Were you happy to marry into the Stone family?"

"At first," Gracie said, and then looked at him. "Did Buck tell you that the first Stone to settle in this area married a woman who was a mail-order bride?"

Calen shook his head. "I didn't know that."

"It's so romantic," Gracie said, a distant smile on her face, and then she seemed to remember the present. "You must be starved."

Calen figured that was his cue to postpone the rest of the discussion. So he asked if she would like him to bless the food. She nodded and he held out his hand.

After a slight hesitation, Gracie nestled her hand in his and he was ready.

Calen bowed his head and closed his eyes. "Father, You have provided for us this morning. You keep us every day, and today is certainly no exception. We ask You to help Renee. Help her body to heal and her spirit to be made aware of Your love for her. Give us strength. We ask You now to bless this food to our bodies—that we may serve You with it. In Jesus's name, Amen."

Calen opened his eyes slowly. He was reluctant to let go of Gracie's hand. He would have thought it might be awkward to sit at this table without Buck, but it wasn't. His boyhood friend was resting in an unmarked plot in the cemetery behind the church in Dry Creek. And, somehow, Calen felt that the better part of Buck would approve of him sitting here, where he could trace the outline of that horse and remember the days of their childhood.

The phone rang then and startled Gracie.

"I need to answer it," she said, and slid her chair back from the table. "It might be something about—" Gracie stopped short of naming his daughter, and nodded toward Tessie to let him know she didn't want to worry the child.

Gracie stood and walked over to the phone that hung on the wall by the door.

"Hello," she said tentatively, and turned to face away from the table, no doubt wanting to spare Tessie any talk of her mother's situation.

Calen knew it wasn't the sheriff on the other end of the phone, because Gracie suddenly looked too stiff for that. And, the only one who might be calling about Renee would be the lawman. So Calen figured Gracie was being polite to some telemarketer.

Just then Calen noticed that Tessie was watching him as she played with her cracker. She was looking at him with even more interest than before. They were making progress.

"I've told you all I know," Gracie finally said, loud enough for Calen to hear. "Don't call me anymore."

Gracie took a minute to turn around after she hung up the telephone.

"Bad call?" Calen asked sympathetically. "I sometimes wonder where they get people to make those calls asking for contributions to this or that."

"They probably get them from the newspapers," Gracie said as she walked back to the table, her stride revealing how upset she was. "That was some reporter. Asking about—" Gracie stopped again and looked at Tessie.

"But why would they be calling here?"

"They heard the rumor that I was expecting company last night," Gracie said, sitting down. "Said they'd heard my light was on, like I was sitting here just waiting for someone. They said they wanted to give me a chance to tell my side of the story, but there is no side for me to tell. I suppose Renee said something about my light being on when she drove in."

"But that's ridiculous." Calen started to rise. "You weren't expecting anyone last night. Did you get a number? I'll call them back and tell them that they are way off base."

"You can't," Gracie said as she unfolded the paper napkin by her plate and calmly spread it on her lap. "They don't know about you."

"Well, I don't care if they know who I am or not."

"It would be best if they didn't discover that just yet," Gracie said, and then she smiled at Tessie.

All of the anger went out of Calen as he

saw the look of affection that passed from the woman to the child.

"We have something more important to worry about than whether or not some newspaper says I'm giving refuge to criminals," Gracie said.

"We can worry about them both." Calen uttered the words before he realized she was right. The family-services people could be coming any day now. The sheriff would have put in the call after he arrested Renee this morning. It wouldn't do for the bunkhouse to be crawling with reporters when the family-services people came. And they could come at any time.

"Don't let the reporters spoil your breakfast," Gracie said then as she passed him the plate of pancakes. "We have a full day ahead of us if we're going to get ready to teach that Sunday-school class tomorrow."

"I'm not—"

"Of course you are," Gracie said with steel in her smile. "If I have to do it, you have to do it, too."

Calen nodded as he put a pancake on his plate. He had been going to say he wasn't working today so he'd have time to do whatever she needed. But he tried not to let Gracie know that he was happy enough with the arrangement. She would enjoy thinking she had coerced him into teaching the class with her. Little did she know, he'd do a whole lot more if she were to ask him. He owed her.

And then it struck him. "But we don't even know what the lesson is about!"

"Marriage." She passed him the butter.

"It can't be about marriage," Calen protested as he took the small plate. "It's for the toddlers and the kindergarten class. They don't care about that stuff."

"Well," Gracie grinned. "Mrs. Hargrove left a message on my phone and said the class is practicing for a skit they're doing for the harvest dinner this coming Friday—"

"Friday! That's right."

Gracie nodded as she cut into her pancake. "Anyway, they're doing Noah's ark, and tomorrow they need to be assigned their mate. So they can climb into the ark, two by two. Mrs. Hargrove said she hoped we could set up pairs who were compatible."

"I suppose it does sound like marriage," he agreed, starting to like the way Gracie looked at things.

"Mrs. Hargrove probably meant that they should be the same height."

"That's about all some couples have in common when they marry," Calen noted, trying to keep his face solemn.

"Well, they'll be paired up for life if they're on that ark," Gracie agreed. "No chance of a reprieve. Until death do they part."

Calen saw Gracie's lips twitch and he suspected she was trying to get a reaction from him, as much as he'd like to get a response from her.

"Marriage shouldn't scare a man." he said. "People get married every day."

"Oh," Gracie said.

She didn't look as amused now, Calen thought. So he continued, "I was jealous of Charley and Mrs. Hargrove, remember? I'm impressed by people who get married. I took the plunge once, remember? It didn't turn out, but I did it."

"Okay," Gracie said uncertainly, eyeing him just as suspiciously as Tessie had earlier.

They were both silent for a moment.

"Well, we don't have to worry about that now," Gracie finally said. "We're only pairing the children up to enter the ark. They won't get married for many, many years."

"I'll look forward to the class." Calen looked down to focus on his plate. Then he realized something. "You're awful cheerful about the whole thing, considering you were so set against teaching that class just a few hours ago."

"Oh, I figured it out," Gracie said as she lifted another forkful of pancake. She was relaxed again. "None of the kids will be there. With the flu going around, they'll be sick. Home in bed. Far, far away from us."

Calen smiled. He should have known Gracie would have a plan. If she was right, there would just be him, her and Tessie in the curtained-off corner of the church basement sitting at those little tables Mrs. Hargrove had made especially for her class. No one would bother the three of them and they could finally get some rest. Maybe have some good conversation. If he remembered right, they might even have juice and crackers.

Then he looked at Gracie again. Maybe she was too confident.

Chapter Seven

The next morning, Gracie stood in front of her bedroom mirror and straightened the sleeves on her good black dress. She usually wore some nice pants and a blouse to church, and would have done so today if she thought any of the children would show up for Mrs. Hargrove's class. At least she could put that worry to rest. She could count on the flu to keep the children away from Sunday school.

It wasn't until midnight that the other worry had popped into her mind and brought her wide awake. She hadn't paid much attention to the reporter who had called, but in going back over the conversation, she clearly remembered him saying his newspaper needed an updated picture of her. She had told him he couldn't have a picture and dismissed it, because she knew no one could sneak up on her at the ranch without Rusty barking.

But she hadn't thought about church. That was a public place and, if they used a high-powered lens, she wouldn't even know someone was aiming a camera at her until it was too late. Her only defense was to wear the black dress so she would look as somber as possible if they did get a shot.

The best way to deal with the press, she had decided, was to give them what they wanted as quickly as possible. If she didn't, then the reporters might dig and discover that Calen was Renee Hampton's father. Which would lead them right to Tessie, and the little girl was having enough nightmares without that.

She glanced over at the toddler. Neither one of them had gotten much sleep last night, but the girl seemed content watching her, so Gracie put on a white pearl necklace and lifted up some earrings.

"Those reporters are going to think I'm so classy they'll be afraid to take my picture," Gracie murmured, just to have something to say to the girl.

Tessie reached out as if she wanted to grab the pearls, but Gracie shook her head.

"We don't have time to play," she said as she daubed a little perfume behind her ear.

Tessie was still watching her, so Gracie

tipped up the perfume bottle again and put a touch behind the girl's ear.

"Ahhh." Tessie giggled.

Gracie had discovered it didn't take much to delight the girl even though it was a bewildering time for her. "Your grandfather is going to think I'm spoiling you."

As she spent more time with Tessie, Gracie became convinced the girl's life had been very limited up to now. Maybe it had been her mother's way of protecting her from that Denny fellow she'd mentioned, the one she'd claimed was her husband. Gracie knew the drill. Teach the child to be quiet and as invisible as possible. Discourage all play, because that was unpredictable. Help the child control her emotions, the good and the bad, for any outburst called attention to them from Denny.

Gracie felt her muscles tighten just remembering her days with Buck.

Right then she heard a vehicle engine and stepped over to look out the window. Calen had said he'd borrow a car from the ranch to take her and Tessie to church, but she was still surprised to see he'd remembered. Not all men paid that much attention to a child seat.

The Elktons had some nice-looking vehicles, Gracie thought as she watched the silver sedan glide down the small hill of her drive.

Apparently, most of the cars had come from the family's son, who was some big-shot politician on the East Coast. From what she'd heard, they even had a Mercedes-Benz gathering dust in the garage at the ranch because no one dared drive it on these rough roads.

She glanced over to where Renee's car sat outside the house. It was far from being a luxury car, but Gracie still worried about leaving it there, exposed to the weather. She decided to ask her sons to put it in the barn after church when they and their wives came over for Sunday dinner. The car was run-down, but Renee might need it before long if things went her way.

Gracie put on a sleek black jacket and stooped down to wrap Tessie in the pink afghan she'd been using to keep her warm. The one thing the girl had from the suitcase in the car that looked suitable for church was a pink velour jumpsuit. Gracie also found a white barrette with pink flowers on it for Tessie's hair.

"You're a regular fashion plate," Gracie said as she lifted the girl up and into her arms. Then Gracie managed to pick up her small black purse, too. She didn't intend to go anywhere without a comb. Not with photographers on the loose. She had securely pinned her hair up today, but the last shot of her in the newspaper had made her look as if she'd just survived a tornado. She was glad the newspaper didn't want to use it again.

The knock on the door signaled that Calen had arrived, and Gracie quickly walked through the living room and into the kitchen. On the way through, she glanced over at the tile counter. She'd cleared everything off of it except the large black Crockpot that held the spaghetti sauce. The dial was set to low, and it would be ready when they got back from church. It gave her satisfaction to have the boys and their families come over for their usual Sunday dinner.

"Here we go," she whispered to Tessie as she opened the back door.

The morning sun was shining through the openings on the sides of the porch. It was bright, but there was no missing Calen. He was standing in a dark gray suit, his feet braced apart as if he was commanding a ship's deck in some high sea. Usually, he wore jeans that were faded from hard work, and shirts with cuffs that had frayed from being washed too many times. Seeing him so confident in this suit made her feel as though she didn't know him.

"You look like a banker," she said to him, and then decided that wasn't the half of it.

The fine stripe in his suit made his brown hair look distinguished. It gave a deeper sheen to his eyes and made the dimples on his cheeks more apparent. It might even have made him look taller. He certainly looked fine, especially with that glint of mischief in his eyes. He knew she was surprised. Even that pearl tack holding his cream silk tie in place against his crisp white shirt was more sophisticated than what she usually saw around here.

"Nothing wrong with a man cleaning up to go to the house of the Lord," Calen said, as though it were nothing.

"You never wear a suit," Gracie said, hoping her quickened breathing wasn't noticeable. Once she got over the initial shock of seeing him like this, it was pleasant. Unsettling, but good.

"Don't tell me you've noticed what I wear to church?" Calen teased, a grin growing on his face. "Have you been watching me?"

"Don't be ridiculous," Gracie replied, wondering if the sunshine was just playing a trick on her eyes. He couldn't really be that handsome. She stepped back so she'd be in the shade. "The clothes on a man's back are just a lot more noticeable than the little bit of cream a woman puts in her coffee."

Calen chuckled and spread his hands in surrender. "Don't get me wrong. It doesn't bother me if you want to notice what I wear. I could use some help in picking out my ties, in fact."

"I've never seen you in a tie—well, until now."

She frowned slightly. Maybe it wasn't just the sunlight that made him seem different. Maybe she needed to change the angle she was looking at him from.

"That's why I need help," he said.

Gracie stepped to the right slightly and focused on his tie. "For a start, you need more color. Maybe a dark green tie or—"

Gracie looked down because Tessie was squirming.

"Purty," Tessie said, as she reached out to touch the pearl tack on Calen's tie.

Calen froze as Tessie leaned close, and he looked to Gracie, his eyes pleading for help. Suddenly, he didn't look like some distant banker. He was Calen, and he desperately wanted to hold his granddaughter if he could do so without frightening her.

Tessie had her tiny hand wrapped around the pearl now.

Gracie inched closer to Calen and bent her

head down to whisper to Tessie. "Do you want to go to Grandpa?"

Tessie brought her hand back quickly and, shaking her head, burrowed as close as she could back to where she'd been, flattened against Gracie.

"It's okay," Gracie said as she comforted the little girl. Then she looked up at Calen apologetically. "Maybe next time."

He nodded, his shoulders slumped. "I had just hoped—"

"I'm sure Tessie will come to trust you," Gracie assured him. "She's just had some bad experiences." She looked down then. "Didn't you, sweetie? Some scary things happened, didn't they?"

She touched the girl's cheek to soothe her. But when Gracie looked up into Calen's eyes, she saw that he had stopped looking at his granddaughter. Instead, he was looking straight at her.

"Not all men are like Buck," he said, his voice low.

Gracie felt the color flood her cheeks and she looked down. "I know that."

"Do you?" Calen challenged her softly.

She was silent.

"I should have called the sheriff on him. That night we talked, I didn't know," he said, his voice stronger. "I wish you would have told me."

"He was my husband."

Calen looked as though he wanted to say more, but Gracie didn't want to talk about it.

"We best get to church," she said as she shifted Tessie into her other arm.

Calen stepped back on the porch so she could walk out of the house. She pulled the door closed behind her and started to walk toward the steps. To Gracie's surprise, she was shaking. Calen had struck too close to the truth. She'd been sorely tempted to ask him to take her away that night. She'd stopped loving Buck by then. But her husband had ruined her ability to trust, and she was uncertain about Calen, too.

She hadn't trusted any man back then. Not a man in blue jeans or a suit or a sheriff's uniform. She had not even trusted the pastor of the church. Or Charley. Her sons were in a different category, but they had been teenagers and were as helpless as she had been.

"Don't you want to lock the door?" Calen asked from where he stood to the side.

He was looking at her strangely.

"No one locks anything during the day," Gracie said, trying to force herself to appear calm. She needed to work on her lack of trust.

"You know that. Besides, Rusty will bark if someone comes."

She did trust her dog, she assured herself. She always had trusted animals.

"Okay," Calen said, not giving up his frown as he glanced in all directions. "I guess I'm just wondering what else is going to happen around here. I wouldn't want anyone to steal that pot of spaghetti I smelled."

Gracie walked down the steps. "The only people who might come around are reporters, and all they probably want is to sort through my trash anyway."

She glanced up as Calen walked down the steps, and her body tensed.

She hadn't changed much over the years, she told herself as Calen went by. Prison had not done anything to ease her hesitancy to trust people. Absorbing that thought, she stood there until she realized what it all meant. She wondered if she even trusted her Father in Heaven. Maybe that's what her resistance to marriage was all about. If she did not trust Him, she could not trust a man if He did happen to send one to her. The spiral of distrust was about more than marriage and had much worse consequences. It affected her entire life, spiritual and social. Maybe her sons were right to be worried about her.

She looked down at Tessie. She hadn't realized she had so much in common with the little girl. The distrust rose up from deep within both of them and affected everything in them.

Calen quickly moved the child seat to the back of the sedan. Then he got Tessie strapped into it. While he did that, Gracie opened the door and sat in the front on the passenger side. Something was bothering her and she was quiet. Not that he knew what it was. Of course, something was bothering him, too. How did a man prove he could be trusted if a woman didn't trust him enough to even let him try?

Words alone would not do it, he knew.

He finally walked around the car and slid into the driver's seat, turning the key in the ignition. The problem was he didn't even understand what made a woman trust a man. For himself, he could size a fellow up pretty quickly on the job. But with women it was different.

Calen backed the car up and turned it around so they could drive into Dry Creek.

He glanced sideways at Gracie. She'd stayed with her husband all those years. Maybe there was something in that to give him a clue.

"Why did you marry Buck anyway?" he

asked as he turned to go onto the gravel road that ran along the property line of the Stone place.

"What?" Gracie looked over cautiously.

She'd been staring out the side window at the dormant fields. There was nothing to warrant a second look, but she had seemed engrossed.

"You must have thought about it," Calen persisted before she could turn her attention away from him. "I know he had a good sense of humor."

"I certainly didn't marry him for that."

The ground had frosted last night and white speckles still remained on the dried grass on both sides of the road. The sun was rising higher in the sky and would be getting warmer as the day wore on.

"I know you needed a home," Calen finally said. He just couldn't leave it alone. He remembered when Gracie had moved to Dry Creek to live with a distant uncle. The old man had taken her in reluctantly and had died a year or so after she'd gotten married. He'd been frail and she'd likely worried about him dying from the day she'd moved into his house.

"I can take care of myself," Gracie protested, but she seemed to be studying him some. He thought she was going to tell him to mind his own business, but she didn't.

Calen decided there was no point in sparing his own feelings. "Was it because you loved him?"

Gracie was silent for a minute before answering. "I thought I did at the time."

Calen swallowed and did not say anything. He had asked the question; he needed to accept her answer.

Then she continued, her voice soft. "Buck was strong and handsome. You remember how he was. I was eighteen and he swept me off my feet. He bought me roses one day and knelt down in the corner of the wheat field here and promised to make me part of his family—the generations of family that were so important to him. He talked about them like they were going to ride in off the range for a drink of water. He knew their names and everything."

Gracie was staring straight ahead, lost in the past.

"His mother didn't like me, though," she said then. "She was still alive those first years we were married. I used to dream of how much better my life would be if she moved out. I didn't realize she was all that was holding Buck back from being the man he was to become."

Calen nodded. Buck had been an only child, and his mother had pushed him to excel in everything. She'd made broad hints to Buck that he should marry a woman who would inherit something. Land or money, she didn't care which. She thought either would give Buck political opportunities. Calen had wondered at the time how the woman would receive a daughter-in-law like Gracie, who had nothing but herself to offer.

"Buck was jealous of you," Gracie said then as she turned to him. "I don't know if you knew that. But that night when you brought him home from the bar, he was so out of it that he didn't know what happened. He thought you'd brought him home so you could be with me. I tried to tell him that we just sat and drank cup after cup of that lemon tea you liked so well. We might have talked for a long time, but that was all there was to it. I was married and my vows were important to me."

"I gave you my phone number that night." Calen never had liked tea or lemons. The fact that he would sit and drink repeated cups of the brew would have been all Buck needed to know. No wonder the man had been jealous. He and Gracie had grown close that night, but neither one of them had crossed any line. Or even acknowledged the feelings they had, sitting around that kitchen table.

Gracie nodded, but didn't say anything more.

By this time, they were making the turn onto the road that would lead them straight into Dry Creek. There wasn't much to the small town, except for a dozen houses and a few businesses, but there was no place Calen would rather be on a Sunday morning than sitting in a church pew there. The road was asphalt, but no sidewalks or parking spaces were to be found. He ran his eyes down the line of buildings on the right side of the road just for the pleasure of it, and then stopped.

Something was wrong.

"There shouldn't be so many people on the side of the road, should there?" He saw women with long black coats and toddlers bundled up in heavy jackets. All of them walking toward the church. He turned to Gracie. "I thought everyone would be home with the flu."

He looked closer. "They're pretty small, those kids."

Gracie's jawline was rigid and her voice quivered ever so slightly as she said, "I didn't think anyone would come to the class."

Gracie was pale by the time she finished talking. She could see the children, too.

"Oh, they're coming, all right," Calen said

as he slowed down the car so he could count them. There were seven children that would be in the right age range. And there would likely be others who had already reached the church.

"They probably don't know Mrs. Hargrove is sick," Gracie muttered, half to herself. "Or, maybe she's gotten better and will be there."

The color was coming back to her face.

"Yes, that's it," Gracie said, looking even more relieved.

Calen didn't have the heart to remind her that Mrs. Hargrove was very conscientious. She would have called Gracie this morning if there had been a change of plans.

Instead, he parked the car on the street beside the church and sat there while Gracie studied the other cars that were parked down the street.

"I don't see Mrs. Hargrove's car," Gracie finally admitted. "Maybe they walked."

He kept silent. Usually people who lived in Dry Creek did walk to church, but Mrs. Hargrove and Charley always drove one of their cars if their arthritis was acting up. And they had needed a car every Sunday for the past year. He watched the same realization occur to Gracie.

"I really do need to teach the class, don't I?" she finally said.

Calen took a deep breath.

"I'll be right beside you," he said, but she had already turned to look out the window again at the forward march of the children going up the stairs to the church.

He doubted she even heard him. He didn't bother repeating it. He figured what he needed to do now was to help her gather up Tessie and get down to the church basement so she could meet their Sunday-school class before chaos reigned. He would worry about impressing her once the hour was over.

He opened the car door and stood outside.

Then he looked down at his clothes— the only suit he owned. He'd wanted to get Gracie's attention, but wearing the suit might have been a mistake. He wondered if the dry cleaners in Miles City could remove orange marker and sticky stuff like glue and anything else toddlers touched.

He turned to where Gracie had stepped out. Because there were no sidewalks, the ground was rough. He walked around the car so he could steady her since she'd worn high heels. "Shall we?"

For a second, he thought she was going to slide back into the car. But she squared her shoulders and nodded her head.

"How bad can it be?" she whispered as she looked up at him.

He didn't bother to answer.

"I like the heels," he said instead, as he put his arm solidly behind her.

"They're for the reporters," she whispered.

"What reporters?"

He had hoped she'd worn them for him.

She looked around. "They'll be here somewhere. Hiding, most likely."

She must be more nervous about the reporters than she was about him, he thought, as she leaned into him and tried to smile.

A smile shouldn't require that much determination, he thought as his heart sank.

It was going to be a long Sunday-school hour.

Chapter Eight

Gracie stopped just before the steps leading up to the church. The sun had risen until it was high in the sky and there were no longer any shadows to the day. The church stood squarely where it always had, the white paint on its outside walls gleaming and its steeple short enough to show the struggle of the congregation to build it. With its brightness, few people looked down to the basement windows, preferring instead to look at the modest stained-glass squares that were seen midway up each side of the church. On the ground, around the building, the dirt was broken here and there by clumps of withered prairie grass, already lying dormant in preparation for a cold winter.

Gracie had been doing her best to look like a woman who relied on a man for every move she made. She'd known women like that, but it didn't come natural to her. She wasn't sure it equaled trust, but she was willing to try it if doing so made Calen feel better.

Then she noticed something was not right. The man's arm still supported her so she knew it wasn't the ground shifting on her. Tessie was not moving in her arms, so that wasn't it. Then she realized that the mothers in their long black coats were coming back down the stairs and they didn't have their children with them.

"Aren't you staying?" Gracie asked, trying not to give in to the alarm that raced through her. She'd thought she could at least send the children out to sit with their parents if the class went badly.

The first mother in line just looked at the cement steps under her feet and shook her head, before moaning incoherently.

That's when Gracie noticed that the women all wore pajamas under their coats. And their hair wasn't combed and their complexions were that pasty pale she'd seen too much of lately.

"We're sick," the second mother in line said, as she stumbled past Gracie with a scarf wrapped around the bottom half of her face as if she could ward off offending germs that way.

The third mother stopped briefly and made eye contact. "We're so grateful you're taking care of our kids. We're going back to bed."

"But I'm not—" Gracie started to say, until she realized no one was listening.

The rest of the women didn't say anything as they filed by, until the final mother stopped.

"You'd better get down there," she said with a note of resigned panic in her voice. "I think the lions are going to attack the rabbits."

"But—" Gracie muttered as she watched all the mothers scurry away, their black coats making them look like a line of retreating ants fleeing from some natural disaster. "I don't think rabbits are even on the list."

She looked up at Calen. His chin was resolute, but his eyes had grown warm with humor.

She dared him to speak and he held his tongue for a few minutes.

"Like the woman said, we better get down there," Calen finally said. She didn't move, so he leaned down and whispered, "At least the mothers are talking to you now."

Gracie swatted his shoulder at that, but her lips did turn up slightly. "I was hoping they'd ask me to help make the table decorations for the harvest dinner. Everybody's doing that."

"Well, not today, they're not," Calen said, and she decided he was right.

Together they climbed the steps up to the church.

"At least I don't run away from my responsibilities," she finally added.

"It'll be fine," Calen said when they reached the top. "We have juice and crackers for them, don't we? We'll just feed them for an hour. Eat. Drink. Be merry. They'll be fine."

"Mrs. Hargrove wants them assigned to their animal roles," Gracie said as she looked around. "She has a list of which animals she wants. I remember lions and elephants. And birds of some kind. Doves, of course. Sheep, I suppose. The list is in my purse."

The church door opened and Elmer Maynard held it for them. Heated air floated out as they walked in. The old man had his white hair slicked back and a silver bolo tie around the neck of his cowboy-cut beige shirt.

"I'm the welcoming committee today," he said, as he managed to hold out a hand for Gracie to shake without letting go of the door. "The Redferns are sick and asked me to fill in for them."

"Doesn't anybody here get the flu shot?" Gracie asked, as she shifted Tessie slightly so she could take his bony hand.

"The flu came early this year." Elmer shook her hand firmly as Calen entered, and the older man let the door close.

"Well, it always comes early," Gracie said, feeling a little testy. Anyone who lived together with others as she had in prison knew a person should not wait until their neighbors got sick before they got the flu shot. It was too late if they did that.

She looked up then. The heavenly sound of piano music was coming from beyond the archway that led into the main part of the church where services would be held after Sunday school. The first few pews were filled with the adult class. Gracie expected her sons and their wives were already there, but she couldn't see them. She looked at her watch. She was a little early.

"Nice tie," Elmer said to Calen, and then chuckled. "Most fellows around here don't put on a tie until they get engaged."

"You're wearing a tie," Gracie reminded him. He'd been a widower for close to twenty years now. "And you're not engaged."

"Bolos are nothing," Elmer said as he flicked the tips of his tie. "It's the big-city ties that show a man's under a woman's fashion influence."

Elmer looked at Gracie, a sly look in his eyes. "You've got a good sense of style."

"Not really," she said, knowing full well what he was implying.

The older man's face lit up in delight.

"I'll send you an invitation to the wedding," Calen offered at the same time, grinning.

"He's not marrying anyone." Gracie shook her head at Elmer. "So don't you start any rumors. He's only trying to give me a hard time."

The older man chuckled at that and hit his leg with his hand to signal his enjoyment.

Men, Gracie told herself, could be relied upon for some things, but none of them good.

Just then a screech came from the basement of the church.

"Oh, we've got to go," she said as she settled Tessie more firmly on her hip.

Calen started through the door to the stairs first, but Gracie was right behind him. Their shoes clattered on the old, worn steps as they rushed down from the foyer of the church to the landing at the bottom, where a door opened out to the main part of the basement.

Calen reached for the bottom doorknob at the same time that Tessie giggled.

"You liked bouncing down the stairs, didn't you, sweetie?" Gracie asked the girl. And then she turned to Calen. "Do you think it's safe to take her into that room? Those kids sound wild."

Calen grunted as he pushed the door open. "She's one of them. She'll fare better than we will."

Gracie followed him through the main part of the basement. All that separated the various classes were long black curtains. They were so worn Gracie wondered sometimes if they were left over from some war effort. Mrs. Hargrove's class had been stationed in the far corner because they were expected to be a little noisier than the older children.

No one thought they would be as loud as they were right now, though, and several of the other teachers were looking out of their classroom areas to see what was wrong.

"We're just late," Gracie apologized as she kept walking as fast as she could. She was beginning to wish she'd worn her tennis shoes instead of her high heels. The sound of her heels as she hurried across the linoleum floor was loud and clicking.

"Those shoes of yours sound very feminine," Calen said as they trotted down the room. How he had breath to talk she didn't know.

"I like it. Tap. Tap. Tap. Tap," he added.

"Your cowboy boots are just as loud," she

managed to say in return, noticing for the first time that he might have changed everything else for today, but his boots were the same ones he wore all the time. That reassured her somewhat, although she wasn't sure why.

They both stopped in front of the curtain that led to Mrs. Hargrove's area and looked at each other.

Then Calen grinned and gestured with his hand. "Ladies first."

Gracie shook her head, but couldn't stop her chuckle. "Coward."

She pushed the curtain aside and faced the chaos. Two boys were standing on the table, hitting each other with cardboard tubes that had probably come from the craft supply cabinet, which stood open. The boys were making some awful noise. She wasn't sure, but she thought they were trying to be elephants. Several of the girls were sitting under the table in a circle eating what she hoped were crackers and singing some senseless song. One lone boy stood at the whiteboard writing the alphabet in blue marker.

None of them even turned to look at Gracie and Calen.

Tessie started to squirm and said, "Me down."

Gracie figured she'd have to give up carrying the girl anyway, so she slid her to the floor and watched her go running off to where the other girls were sitting. Apparently Calen had been right that she'd be welcomed right into the circle.

"Can I have your attention?" Gracie said then, making sure she was smiling at the children as Mrs. Hargrove would want her to do.

The children ignored her. Then Calen put his fingers to his lips and gave a shrill whistle.

"Listen up," he said in a gruff tone that Gracie figured must be his ranch-foreman voice. "We've got work to do, so everybody pay attention. I'm only going to say this once."

The boys stopped growling at each other, although they kept swinging their cardboard trunks. Only one of the girls stopped singing, and she looked up to say, "We couldn't find the juice."

The boy at the whiteboard turned to Gracie then. "There is no juice. We drank it all last week, and Mrs. Hargrove didn't get any more for us."

The two boys stopped swinging at each other and focused on Gracie. She figured she'd found the right word to bring order to this place. They all loved the older woman.

"Mrs. Hargrove asked me to look after you," Gracie said, thinking she was being very diplomatic. "I've got a lesson to tell you about and everything. I'll do my best to do things just the way she would."

"You got any juice?" The boy with the marker started writing on the board again. "She'd bring us our juice."

Gracie wondered if maybe the older woman's name wasn't the key to silence after all. Maybe it was the beverage.

"I told them I could go get us all coffee," the taller of the dueling boys said. "There's a big pot made upstairs. It wouldn't take nothing to bring down a pitcher full of it."

Gracie had visions of hot-water burns and livid parents. "No one is to go near the coffeepots—ever. You shouldn't even be drinking coffee."

One of the girls looked up. "Not even when we're old like you are?"

Gracie had forgotten how specific one needed to be with children. "Line up. Hands at your sides. We're going to count down."

Gracie had heard those directions enough in life that they were naturally the ones she chose in her moment of crisis.

"Are we going to play prison?" the boy with the marker said, and she had no idea how he knew that was a jailhouse routine.

"No one plays prison," she assured him. "I just want us to line up."

He looked disappointed.

Calen whistled again and, this time, the children started to obey. They lined up as best they could and then turned to her, their innocent faces trusting that she had something planned.

She was silent.

Finally Calen leaned over and whispered, "We can't make them stand like that the whole hour."

"You heard them," Gracie whispered back. "There's no juice. We'll have mutiny on our hands if we give them an inch."

She had learned some things in prison. She looked and noticed that Tessie had lined up with the other children, looking happy.

"You didn't study the lesson, did you?" Calen kept his voice low so only she could hear him.

"Well, they weren't supposed to be here," Gracie snapped back. "They were supposed to be sick."

Calen nodded and started looking around. "There has to be a Bible here. I'll read the story of Noah's ark to them. That's probably what the lesson book would say to do anyway."

"Anyone know where the Bible is?" Gracie asked when Calen didn't find anything at first glance.

"Mrs. Hargrove tells us the story without reading the Bible," one of the girls said. "She uses different voices, too. And animal sounds, too. Once she made lightning."

"Well, I'm just going to tell it to you straight," Gracie said, as she motioned for Calen to come back. The Bible wouldn't be in the craft supply cabinet. She knew Mrs. Hargrove wouldn't allow that.

"Are you going to tell us a prison story?" the boy who'd been at the whiteboard asked.

Gracie decided he was all too interested in jails.

"No," she said firmly. "I'm going to tell you about the ark that Noah built."

"I bet he had bars on the windows of that ark," the boy said, undeterred.

Gracie realized she didn't know. She'd never heard anyone talk about Noah's windows before. She supposed they had something to keep things out at night. There was no glass, of course, but maybe he had shutters of some kind. There may even have been wooden bars.

"Did he?" the littlest of the girls asked, her voice wavering. "Were the animals in prison when they were in the ark?"

"I don't want to be in prison," another girl said and started to wail.

"My mother will kill me if I go there," one of the boys muttered, looking worried.

"No one is going to prison!" Gracie said loudly. It wasn't really a shout, she told herself. But it did stun the children into silence. And it surprised her. Only Tessie seemed unaffected; she smiled serenely as she sat down on the floor and pulled the barrette out of her hair.

At least the children were quiet, though, Gracie congratulated herself, until she heard someone clear their throat and she turned.

One of the other teachers had put her head around the curtain. "Everyone okay?"

"Yes, yes, we're fine," Gracie told the woman, as she smoothed a stray strand of hair back from her face. What was the woman's name again? "Just fine."

The other teacher looked skeptical, but she smiled. "Good."

Gracie knew the woman was ready to leave, and she didn't want to think about the rumors that could be spread.

"We're playing prison," the boy from the whiteboard announced in satisfaction.

The woman's mouth made a perfect O.

"No, no," Gracie gulped. "We're just getting ready to talk about Noah's ark."

Calen came to stand beside her then and smiled at the woman.

"You know how kids are, Mary," he said, his voice confident and easy.

Mary Miller was the woman's full name, Gracie remembered.

"We might talk a bit about Apostle Paul's time in prison if we get done with the story of Noah," Calen added. "The boys like that."

"Oh, yes, of course," the other teacher said as she smiled. "Well, carry on."

The woman stepped back and the curtain fell into place.

"Look what I found," Calen said as he lifted a dusty bottle of grape juice from the floor. "It was behind the Bethlehem star they use in the Christmas pageant."

He blew the dust off the lid. "It will be as good as new."

"Well, if we find some cups," Gracie said in relief. "We can have some juice and crackers."

"It should be bread and water," the boy with the prison fixation muttered, but Gracie didn't pay any attention to him this time. She wanted a cup of juice herself and she was going to have it.

Calen passed the last of the crackers around. So far, twenty minutes of the Sunday-school time had been served. He knew because a large clock hung above the supply cabinet marking down the hour.

Gracie sat on one of the children's chairs. She was rubbing her temples as though she had a headache.

"Do you have that list Mrs. Hargrove gave you that tells what animals were going into the ark?" Calen figured he could get the class started at least. He knew how to organize a spring cattle drive for the Elkton Ranch with a thousand head of bawling cattle and two dozen sleepy cowhands. He could manage an ark and eleven little kids who were only pretending to be animals.

"Oh," he realized then. "Is someone missing from the class?"

The children looked at him blankly. Finally, one of them said, "Mrs. Hargrove."

"No, I mean there are five pairs of animals and one left," he said.

"We all have to be in a pair," a little girl said, as she frowned. "Mrs. Hargrove said."

"It's Tessie," Gracie roused herself enough to say. "But maybe we can have three of something. Maybe three lizards. They don't really pair up anyway."

"Why not?" one of the dueling boys asked,

as he gave a crooked grin to that same little girl. "Don't they fall in love?"

"I don't like lizards." The girl scowled at the boy and blinked back a tear. "I'm going to be a bunny. Lizards are icky."

"You're the one that's icky," the boy retaliated.

"That's it," Calen said, his voice sharp enough to stop everyone. He turned to the boy. "We don't call anyone icky in this class. And we don't make fun of anyone, even lizards. You're going to eat everyone's dust for that remark. You'll pull up the rear of this cattle drive."

"Did Noah have cows?" one of the other girls asked, her mouth wide. "We have cows on our ranch."

Calen nodded, even though he didn't know. "Since he had two of everything, I'd say probably. Cattle are an important part of the animal kingdom."

He figured he owed that endorsement to the local ranchers.

Then he looked over at Gracie, and she was still sitting down at the table and pouring herself another cup of juice. That had been three cups so far, but he wasn't going to say anything. Her face was so pale he figured she needed the extra shots of vitamins.

Calen was feeling pleased with himself for taking the burden of organizing off Gracie's back when she looked up at him, a stricken expression on her face.

She got up from the table, stepped close to him and lowered her voice. "You don't think this juice could have fermented, do you?" Gracie lifted a small paper cup of the grape liquid. "It tastes a little off."

"You only just now noticed?" Calen asked. He hadn't had any of it.

Gracie shrugged.

Just then one of the boys hiccupped.

"Don't even think it," Calen said as he looked at the clock. They had thirty minutes left. "Just put the cap back on the bottle. We'll throw the rest away."

Gracie nodded.

"Let's number off," Calen continued. "Boy. Girl. One. One. Two. Two."

The children looked at him blankly.

"I don't think they know how to count yet," Gracie finally whispered. "At least, not like that with the double numbers."

"What are we going to do?" he asked then.

Gracie didn't consider for more than a second. "Go upstairs and get Cat—you know, Jake's wife. Tell her I need her down here."

"Oh," Calen said, not moving. He refused

to point out that he had been the one to find the Bible. He had been the one to find the old bottle of juice. And, even if the juice thing had not turned out quite so well, he had been here for Gracie. "You can trust me to help. You don't need Cat."

"I—" Gracie looked up at him, her face showing the emotions racing across her mind. She was embarrassed at being caught. "It's just—you know, men—"

Then he saw it. Guilt. He'd called it straight that she didn't trust him, whether to stay or be useful, he didn't know.

"Is that all men you don't trust or just me?" he asked, but she didn't answer. "Don't worry. I'll go find one of the older kids from Mary's class to ask Cat to come down. But I'm not leaving you here with this zoo—no matter what you think."

"Oh," Gracie said then, looking unsettled by that statement, as if she didn't know whether that was good or bad.

"Now, everybody line up by height." Calen turned from her to speak to the children. "I want you all to have a partner by the time I get back. Pick someone who's close to you in height and stand next to them. Take each other's hands so we'll know you are a pair."

Calen drilled into the eyes of the boy who

had been in trouble most of the class since his "icky" remark.

"And you." He pointed at the boy so there would be no misunderstanding. "You pair up with her."

Calen indicated the little rabbit girl, who blinked at him when she realized what he'd said. She looked as if he'd thrown her to the wolves, but he figured it would be good for her to learn to be a little braver, just as the boy could stand to be more tolerant.

"But we're not the same height," the girl ventured to say timidly.

"Work it out," Calen said, just as he'd tell his ranch hands.

Amazingly, the children looked as though they were going to obey, even the boy with the attitude. So Calen ducked around the curtain and went in search of someone to send upstairs for reinforcements. It was disheartening that Gracie didn't trust him to handle a problem this simple when even the little rabbit girl was willing to go along.

He had always thought Gracie was just independent, but now he was wondering if she had enough trust left in her to be close to any man again. There were always walls. He knew that well enough. But he couldn't just demand trust; if it wasn't freely given, it wasn't there at all.

Father, we need Your help with this, he prayed as he walked. *At least, I need Your help.* Gracie probably felt she was doing fine, he told himself. *Oh, and help the little rabbit girl, too. Give her courage.*

Chapter Nine

Gracie was sitting in a pew, with Tessie snuggled next to her, safe in the blessed silence that surrounded her. The Sunday-school hour had finally ended, with each child assigned a role in the skit for Friday's harvest dinner. And all of the adults, except for her, were now in the back reception area having a final cup of coffee or tea before coming back into this part of the church for the eleven o'clock worship service.

Even more importantly, someone, generally the father, had come to pick up each one of the youngsters from the class area. Disaster had been averted. She'd emptied the juice bottle and put it in the trash. She'd swept up the cracker crumbs and the torn tissues Tessie had left behind. She'd checked to be sure the one little girl was doing okay with the boy

Calen had forced her to pair with, and saw she had stopped crying.

Gracie worried briefly about costumes, until the boy who was so interested in prisons had told her that Mrs. Hargrove had paper masks and colored blankets for them to wear to represent the different animals.

And now Gracie sat here with the sun streaming down on her face as it came through the stained-glass windows. She wondered briefly if the reason Mrs. Hargrove enjoyed her class so much was because of this sweet feeling of relief when it was over for another week.

Tessie stirred beside her and Gracie straightened up to look around some more. An oak pulpit stood at the front of the church and a mauve carpet spread out from beneath it, running between the pews until it reached the wide door to the outside. She suddenly remembered the many times she'd seen brides walk down that carpeted path. They were visions of loveliness.

"Oh," Gracie muttered to herself in disgust. She hadn't expected the reminder of brides to bring her back to earlier thoughts about trust. How could something so lacy and lovely turn on her? The sun wasn't so comforting anymore.

Fortunately, Calen was not there to make

her feel worse. She knew well enough that taming the children had not been her biggest challenge of the day. She had failed in some major way this morning and it had nothing to do with the story of Noah, unless one considered that God had asked Noah to do something so difficult it had seemed impossible.

Almost as impossible as her trusting Calen to support her in the Sunday-school class.

She knew the man wanted her to trust him, but how could she? He was asking for more than trust just for this morning, too. Where would she be if she went around trusting every man who asked her to?

Gracie looked up and saw that someone had walked to the piano with a hymnal in her hands. When the woman turned her head, she could see it was Doris June. Mrs. Hargrove's middle-aged daughter wore a navy suit and her blond hair was perfectly in place. When Gracie looked closely, though, she could see that the other woman's face was pale and drawn. She seemed determined to substitute for her mother at the piano. If Gracie knew Mrs. Hargrove, the older woman had threatened to come and play herself unless someone volunteered to take her place.

Anyone could trust Doris June to help them in their time of need.

Gracie wished she felt the same way about Calen. And maybe she should, she told herself. Calen was as upstanding as Doris June. He had never failed anyone, except perhaps the wife he'd had long ago. But even Doris June had made early mistakes in love.

No, Gracie trusted one and not the other. And the difference was solely that Calen was a man. Realizing her prejudice made her feel small.

She certainly wished she did trust him. She glanced down at Tessie as the girl blissfully tore apart another tissue. But wanting to trust someone didn't make it so. *Am I wrong, Father?* She sat there and acknowledged the likelihood of it. *Help me if I am.*

Gracie sat up on the edge of the pew, poised to stand if she needed. The very thought of asking God to make her trust more made her feel as though someone might suddenly ask her to jump off a cliff and tell her they would catch her at the bottom.

Lord, maybe just one small step of trust, she prayed then, just to remind God that she probably wasn't going to be very good at this. *And if You could hold my hand, I'd appreciate it.*

She heard several voices then. People were starting to come into the main part of the church. Before long, her oldest son, Wade, slipped into the pew beside her. Now she had her son on one side and Tessie on the other.

"I don't know if you've seen this," Wade said, as he unfolded the Billings newspaper he'd been carrying in front of his Bible. "One of the Elkton ranch hands got it in Miles City this morning."

"Oh, dear," Gracie said.

There, in a corner of the front page, was a photo of her. She suddenly wished she had told the reporter yesterday that he could come right out to the ranch and shoot as many pictures as he wanted. Instead, the paper had used a picture of her that she hadn't known about. They had clearly shot this one after her sentencing a decade ago. Her face was twisted in grief because she'd just said goodbye to her sons. Her hair didn't look like a tornado this time, but it was flattened to her head as if she'd been in a flood. Her hands were handcuffed behind her back, and two deputies were forcefully helping her into the patrol car. She even had a spot of something, coffee maybe, on the sleeve of her blouse.

"Can you read it to me?" she asked her son, blinking back the sudden tears. "I guess I do need glasses."

She did trust her sons, she thought to herself. That was something.

Wade looked at her a moment and then nodded. "We can read it later. It just says that Renee Hampton, suspected in the robberies in northern Montana, was arrested on your porch last night. And that you had no comment."

"Saying I had no comment makes me sound like I have something to hide," Gracie fretted. Leave it to those reporters. "I didn't say 'no comment' exactly, I said it was none of their business."

Wade didn't say anything. He just put his arm around her shoulders.

Calen sat down in the last row of pews just as the pastor called for the first hymn to be sung. Before he knew it, Doris June was pounding out the tune of "Rock of Ages" on the piano.

It was a comforting song and Calen let it wash over him. He'd known disappointment in his life and he had always survived. He'd do it this time, too. After all, it wasn't as if Gracie had ever deceived him. Even in high school, she had never flirted with him the way the other girls did. She'd been serious back then, devoted to her Buck. He supposed when her heart had broken over her marriage, it had broken for good.

It was not surprising she couldn't open her feelings up enough to trust him.

Maybe, in time, he would suggest the two of them become friends, he told himself. But not now. His dream had to die first, even if he hadn't known until today that it still had such a strong hold on his heart.

It was ironic that it took facing that Gracie would never trust him enough to love him before he admitted, even to himself, how much he had envied Buck Stone back then. His friend had family going back for generations, but, except for his widowed mother, Calen only had himself. It never had been fair.

But, for now, he'd keep his feelings to himself, because although he'd had no relatives in the past, now he had Renee and Tessie. Gracie had invited him to her place for dinner after church, and he planned to go. No matter how things stood between him and her, he needed to get to know Tessie better. She and his daughter had to be number one in his life.

He'd taken some wrapped mints from the coffee table earlier, and he planned to see whether Tessie would come to him if he had some candy for her. It wasn't the way he'd like it to happen, but if she came to him for any reason he'd be grateful. Until she did, she'd have to stay with Gracie. He didn't want to frighten his granddaughter.

In any event, he'd start working on a place for them to live. After dinner at the Stones', he planned to go back to the cook's quarters beside the bunkhouse and take a scrub brush to everything in sight. The crew didn't have a cook right now, and he figured that was the best place for him and Tessie until he could buy a trailer and pull it onto the ranch. He wasn't sure when the state family-services representative would show up, but the sheriff had warned him that they liked to make surprise visits. Calen figured cleanliness was the minimum they would expect. If any stores were open in Miles City today, he would drive over and pick up a doll for Tessie. The sheriff was likely right about that, too. The representative would expect at least one toy.

By the time the hymn was over, Calen wondered how he was going to be able to do it all.

Because so many of the women had the flu, the pastor asked for extra volunteers to help make tissue flowers for the tables at Friday's dinner. Calen expected Gracie to raise her hand, since that's what she had mentioned wanting to do, but she gave no indication she would volunteer.

The rest of the announcements went smoothly.

A list of names was read, remembering those suffering from the flu, and the pastor prayed they would all get well.

The sermon passed in a blur. Calen's eyes kept being drawn to the pew where the Stone family sat together. He was surprised Gracie hadn't eased up on her distrust of men when she was surrounded by so much family love. Wade sat on one side of her, his wife, Amy, next to him. Amy was due to give birth to their first child any day now. Then on the other side of Gracie sat Tessie, and then Jake Stone with his wife, Cat, and their daughter, Lara. Gracie's youngest son, Tyler, sat a little farther down on the pew with his pregnant wife, Angelina.

Apparently, Gracie's lack of trust didn't extend to her sons, Calen thought. Not that he wished it did. Her sons were all decent, Christian men and were doing what they could to bring the Stone family ranch back to its rightful state. The cattleman in him appreciated that, especially since they were going to run an Angus breed when they got things going.

Before long, the church service was over and Calen was standing up to shake hands with people as they all milled around. He knew trouble was coming, though, when he saw Mary Miller, one of the Sunday-school teachers, walk over to him as he was trying to make his way to the back of the church so he could slip out the door.

"Mr. Gray," Mary gushed a little as she waved a hand at him. She was a birdlike woman in her mid-sixties and breathless. "I'm sorry to keep you, but if you have a minute—"

Mary fluttered close to him before he could answer. And by the time he looked up, three of the other women in the Sunday school had joined her.

"Now, you know my name's Calen," he said, hoping to remind them all that they had known him for decades. They might not be friends, but they were certainly good acquaintances.

"Well, yes," Mary said as her face grew a little pink. "It's not often we have a man join us downstairs in the Sunday-school room, though."

Calen felt his muscles relax. "No need to thank me. The boys should have more men there teaching them."

"That's just it," one of the other women said, with a quick look at Mary. "Our boys need direction. They're—"

It took Calen a minute to realize there was something more than a simple thank you on the women's minds. They kept glancing at each other as if they were waiting for the others to put some request into words.

"I'm not really in a position to teach every week." He'd taken a guess at why they wanted to talk to him. He knew how much time it took to prepare now, though. And he did have a ranch to run. And with Tessie and Renee, he just couldn't make a commitment now.

"Oh, no, that's not it," one of them said, at the same time as Mary turned around and saw Gracie.

"Oh, Mrs. Stone," Mary called out, and motioned for Gracie to come over as well.

"No point in repeating ourselves," Mary said, her voice high with excitement as if she had an announcement to make.

That sounded ominous to Calen. Especially when the older woman's call to Gracie was overheard by others and, before Gracie even got there, a half dozen of the young mothers had joined the circle. In fact, as he looked around, every woman in the church who wasn't home with the flu was drawing close to the conversation.

This couldn't be good, he thought to himself, remembering the coolness Gracie reported experiencing from these same women.

Gracie gave him a questioning look, but she kept on coming.

Calen almost motioned for her to stay back, but he was afraid that would only draw more attention to them.

"Mrs. Stone has company for dinner," Calen said, doing the next best thing to distract them. These women understood the demands of hospitality. "Maybe we could talk on the phone later this week."

"Nonsense." Gracie had drawn up to the group by now and her voice didn't flinch. Her eyes were flashing, and she shot a look at Calen that told him she would hold him responsible, but she didn't look inclined to back down.

He was proud of her.

He could only hope that the sight of Tessie in Gracie's arms would make the women have some compassion for them.

"I don't suppose any of you know how to help a toddler who has fears?" he asked then. If anything would distract them, if would be a sweet-faced child like Tessie.

Fortunately, Tessie played her part by grinning at the women.

Mary looked at the girl. "She doesn't look afraid of much to me."

He realized then that none of the women probably knew who the girl was.

"Besides, it was because of the children that we wanted to talk to you," one of the young mothers said then. Calen scrambled to remember the woman's name. He didn't know all of the young couples in the church, and this family had moved here only a few months ago. Come to think of it, she was a single mother.

"Mrs. Drake?" he asked.

She nodded and then he remembered. Her son had been the one standing at the whiteboard in class and asking all those questions about prison.

"Does anyone think they can tell us how old Tessie here is?" Calen said, desperately trying to find something to draw their attention away from what he strongly suspected was coming.

All he accomplished was to have them look at him blankly.

"Why don't you know how old she is?" Mary asked suspiciously. "Whose child is she, anyway?"

Calen looked over at Gracie then, only to see her bite her bottom lip in worry.

"I'm afraid I have to be going," Gracie said, looking down and shifting Tessie in her arms.

Calen knew his granddaughter was the only thing that would make Gracie back down, and he was sorry he had led the women in that direction.

Gracie continued, "Dinner is cooking and I need to put some bread in the oven. I truly am sorry about this morning's Sunday-school class, but Mrs. Hargrove asked me and, well, it will never happen again."

Gracie turned before she gave anyone time to respond and started walking to the open door.

Calen turned to follow her. He'd rather face a stampeding herd of cattle than come up against those Sunday-school women again.

He must have had his head down, because he sure didn't see anyone standing in the doorway to the church until Gracie stopped right in front of the man and gave a yelp of distress.

"What's wrong?" Calen took two large steps to bring himself even with Gracie. "Did you drop something?"

That's when Calen saw the man raise the camera to his eye.

Gracie bent to set Tessie on the floor before the man could get in position, but then she rose up to her full height and faced him like royalty.

"Do your best," Gracie said as she smiled at the photographer.

The flash surprised Calen until he saw that the man with the camera was about his age. Maybe he was more familiar with print than with digital pictures.

To Calen's surprise, Gracie didn't move when the man let his camera hang from the cord around his neck and took a small notebook out of his coat pocket.

"I have a few questions," the reporter said.

Gracie nodded. "I figured you would."

Calen cheered Gracie on as she stood there and answered the man's questions. She told him that she hadn't known Renee Hampton before she showed up on her porch, but that she would have helped anyone in need.

Gracie kept talking to the reporter, but the man never asked about Tessie, so it seemed he gave no thought to her. Tessie, for her part, stayed close to where she had been set on the floor. Calen didn't breathe easy until the man turned and left.

Calen stepped closer to Gracie once the reporter was gone.

"Shall we go home?" he asked, and was relieved when Gracie nodded.

"But, Mrs. Stone," several voices called out, but neither Calen nor Gracie turned.

Instead, Gracie bent down and picked Tessie up. Together she walked with him down the church steps that they had climbed up not more than two hours earlier. When they reached the ground, Calen looked around. "The reporter's gone."

Gracie looked back at the church door. "And the women aren't following."

"Thank God for that," Calen said.

"And thank you," Gracie said.

"What for?" Calen figured he had failed, so he wasn't sure what she was talking about.

"For just being there," Gracie whispered, so low he almost didn't hear it.

Calen stepped closer and put his arm around Gracie's shoulders.

He knew it wasn't a commitment to anything. But it was a glimmer of hope. And that's all he needed for now.

"Let's go home, shall we?" he said as they started to walk back to the car. They could use a peaceful dinner with Gracie's family.

"I hope the spaghetti sauce is doing okay," she muttered when they reached the car.

"I'm sure it's fine," Calen said, as he opened the back door for her to put Tessie in her child seat.

"It better be," Gracie said as she strapped the girl in. "Something needs to go right today."

Calen smiled as he opened the passenger

door for her. Something had already gone right for him. Gracie had thanked him for being there.

Chapter Ten

Gracie leaned her head back against the leather seat in the sedan that Calen was driving. The sky outside had turned gray while they had been inside the church. Clouds were gathered on the horizon behind them as they went down the gravel road away from Dry Creek. She turned to check on Tessie and saw that the toddler was drowsy.

"I wonder when she naps." Gracie turned to Calen with that sudden thought. "I never asked Renee when Tessie takes her nap. I'd forgotten that she probably has a nap time."

"Right after lunch."

Gracie looked at him skeptically. "How do you know?"

"I had a chance to ask Renee when we saw her in the hospital. I also asked about any vaccinations Tessie might have had, but she hasn't had any. I thought I'd take her to the doctor when I get her settled and see about those kinds of things. Renee hasn't been able to afford regular care for Tessie."

"Oh," Gracie said. She should have thought of some of those questions herself.

"And she likes curly fries," Calen added with a grin as he turned to Gracie. "Not that they're that good for her."

"No, no, I suppose not."

Gracie realized that Calen was involved in planning Tessie's care, but it didn't make her rejoice or step back from wanting to be the one to see that the girl had all she needed. Anyone could do well in a sprint, she told herself to justify her feelings. But parenting was a marathon. How would Calen be doing a month from now?

She suddenly realized that Calen's qualifications had nothing to do with her hesitation, though. She didn't want Tessie to go to someone else, even if the girl had adequate care with them.

Lord, what is wrong with me? She looked out the window at the passing fields. *Am I that lonely?*

She saw one or more of her sons every day. And, while she saw less of her new daughters-in-law, she did like them and they came to dinner on Sundays. Jake's daughter, Lara, was in school, so she didn't see much of her. Maybe it would be better when Wade and Amy had their baby, she consoled herself. Maybe she'd be able to care for the little one when Amy went shopping. And, before she knew it, Tyler and Angelina would have their baby, too. She'd have lots of children around.

Calen reached down to turn some knobs on the dash of the car and a burst of classical music filled the car.

"Nice," she said as she turned back from looking out the window. The sound system was very good.

Gracie realized she needed someone to need her. Maybe she should take in boarders, she thought to herself.

"Bach," Calen said quietly.

She looked over at Calen. "I never knew you liked Bach."

Calen chuckled at that. "I read the composer on the CD before I put it in. I figure one of the Elktons bought the thing. I'm more into gospel and country music."

Gracie smiled as she nodded. That sounded like the Calen she knew. He had loosened his tie as well. And completely removed the tie tack and put it somewhere. His hair was a little ruffled from the breeze they had encountered on their way to the car earlier.

She liked him being himself.

The turn to the road that led to her house came all too soon for Gracie. Maybe she needed to just get out and drive around if she was lonely, she told herself. She'd been brooding about people accepting her for too long. This morning at church, she'd realized the women in Dry Creek were unlikely to ever warm up to her. So, she'd go into Miles City and see if she could meet some friends there. Maybe at the new beauty shop there. The world was bigger than Dry Creek.

Before she knew it, the sedan was going over the rise in the driveway to her house. Gracie had always liked that little bump in the road. A person could look down and see the whole Stone ranch spread out in front of them. They could even see the lilac bushes, their bare branches spreading out past the barn.

She never got tired of coming home to this place. While it was Buck's ancestors who had built the ranch, she had grown to love it, too. She sat on the enclosed porch some nights and watched the sunset with Rusty by her side.

She frowned then. The car made the usual amount of vehicle noise. "I don't see Rusty, do you?"

She turned to Calen and he shook his head. Then he rolled down the window on his side of the car, probably hoping to hear better. "Maybe he's out chasing a rabbit or something."

"Maybe," Gracie said as she rolled down her window, too. Cold air came inside, but that didn't stop her from leaning out the window. "Rusty!"

She listened carefully and there was still no response.

"He never goes that far," she said as she looked out to the far field behind the barn.

"I'll go out and call for him while you carry Tessie inside the house," Calen said, a small frown on his weathered face.

"It's just that he never—" Gracie started.

"I know," Calen said gently. "He guards the place when you're gone. He always has."

Gracie pressed her hands together while Calen finished driving the car to the house. She didn't like to think about what might have happened.

"I shouldn't have left him," she whispered finally.

"You can't keep a dog like that wrapped up in cotton," Calen said. "He's probably coming up from the coulee as we speak."

"I expect so," Gracie said in relief. She'd

forgotten that she couldn't see the coulee from here.

"He might be getting a little deaf, too," Calen added as he stopped the car and pulled out the key. "How old is he now?"

"Old enough," Gracie said. Maybe she should have his hearing checked.

"I'll get your door," Calen said as he opened his.

Gracie let him walk around. She was tired. They were all getting old, right along with Rusty.

Calen swung her door open and stepped to the side so he could open the back door and get Tessie as well. He had the girl's seat belt unbuckled by the time Gracie stood up and stepped over to slide the child out.

"I'll just walk you inside," Calen said then.

"But Rusty—"

"He'll come quicker if I have some dog biscuits," Calen said, and she agreed.

She followed Calen up the steps. He'd opened the door and frozen. She could tell by the stillness of his shoulders that something had changed.

She tightened her grip around Tessie. "What's wrong?"

Calen knew someone had been inside Gracie's house the minute he swung the door open to the kitchen. There was a sweaty scent in the air that had not been there earlier. Even with the spaghetti sauce, he could still smell it. He pushed the door a little more and that was when he saw it. Someone had left a battered Kewpie doll dangling from the light above the kitchen table. It was the kind of doll that had been common at the state fair years ago and now was found at garage sales. This one had a string around its neck like a noose and it hung there limply.

He swallowed and knew what he had to do.

"Oh, I forgot to get the keys from Mrs. Hargrove," he said loudly enough for anyone hiding nearby to hear him. "I'm afraid we need to go back and get them."

He closed the door and turned to Gracie. She was standing on the porch with Tessie in her arms and a puzzled look on her face. He put his finger to his lips so she wouldn't say anything.

"Come," he whispered as he took her arm and led her back to the car.

"Don't worry about the child seat," he said quietly as he opened the door for her. "Just hold Tessie. We're not going far."

And they needed to get away.

Calen walked as fast as he dared around to the driver's side of the car. He didn't want to tip anyone off if they were watching. He opened the door and slid behind the wheel without bothering with his own seat belt. He turned the key and was thankful for the power of the engine as it started.

He turned the car around and drove to the top of the rise before he said anything.

"Something's wrong," he said then. "Someone has been in your house."

"Oh, it was probably just one of the boys," Gracie muttered, her relief obvious. "They probably wanted to get some gloves or something. You never know with them. They'll always treat that place like home."

Calen shook his head as he looked in the rearview mirror. "It wasn't one of your sons."

Gracie put her hand on Tessie's back as though to protect the child. "How do you know?"

"Was there a Kewpie doll in the house? You know those plump, little dolls. Maybe in a drawer someplace. This one looked like it was rubber and has seen better days. They used to have them at carnivals for prizes in the shooting games. This one's small, about four inches high with a red gingham dress and a white apron. Yellow hair pulled back in a long braid."

"No," Gracie said, puzzled. "Unless one of

the boys had one up in their rooms. Although I can't imagine any of them having a doll. Besides, they certainly never took part in any shooting games when they were small. Buck didn't like us going out in public."

Calen nodded as he started the car again. "I think we should go wait by the main turnoff. We'll get one of your sons to call the sheriff."

"But why would any—" Gracie began, and then stopped. She looked down at Tessie. "It must be one of those reporters. They'll do anything to get a story."

Calen kept his hands on the wheel. "It's some twisted reporter, if that's the case."

Gracie waited until he turned onto the main gravel road.

"What did you see?" she asked him. "Besides the doll. And don't tell me it was nothing. I have a right to know."

Calen drove the car off the side of the road and parked. Then he turned to Gracie. "I know you have a right. I just can't figure it out. Someone left a Kewpie doll like the one I described hanging from your light over the table."

"But what would it be doing there?"

Calen didn't want to say, but she was right that she was entitled to know. "I'd guess it was meant to frighten you."

Gracie was quiet for so long that he didn't think she was going to respond.

Finally she said, "When I was away in prison, someone came by our house and threw rocks at it. Broke out most of the windows on the one side. I always figured it was some boys looking for target practice." She looked up at him. "It was easier to think that instead of the other option—that someone had that much malice in their heart toward me and my family."

"But why would anyone do something now?" Calen said. "You've been back almost a year."

"There was a story in the Billings paper this morning," Gracie said calmly. "It wasn't a large one, but Wade showed it to me. Maybe whoever did it lives a little farther out and didn't know I was back. Every time anything gets published, people start thinking about it again. Some people still think I got away with murder."

"But you didn't kill Buck," Calen protested as he turned around to look at her fully. "Old man Mitchell confessed before he died. And Tilly told what she knew. Surely no one thinks you had anything to do with it anymore."

There were times in a man's life when he needed to put his own hurts and desires aside,

Calen thought, and now was such a time for him. He might be disappointed that Gracie did not turn to him with the trust he would like to see on her face. But he could no more stop himself from reaching out his hand and touching her face than he could stop himself from breathing. He used his thumb to wipe away the tear that ran down her cheek.

Then he kissed her lightly on her lips.

She drew in her breath and stopped for a moment.

"People believe in all kinds of conspiracies," Gracie said as she looked away from him. She did not move her face from his hand, though, and for that he was grateful. If anything, she leaned deeper into his hand. "I can guarantee there are a few around Dry Creek who think I paid Mr. Mitchell to say what he did. After all, he was dying by the time he confessed. Everyone knew he'd never serve any time for the murder. Maybe he had need of a few thousand dollars."

"But—"

Gracie stopped him. "No, it could have happened that way. You're kind to defend me, but people have their opinions."

Just then a horn honked and they both looked up. A black pickup was coming down the road on the opposite side.

"That will be Wade," Gracie said. "He and Amy never stay too long after the service. Now that she's so far into her pregnancy, she likes to go home and rest a bit before she comes over to my place for dinner." Gracie paused and looked to him in alarm. "My spaghetti sauce. No one unplugged that Crockpot, did they?"

Calen tried to remember, but couldn't. "I don't think I saw a cord dangling from the counter, but if they'd been neat about it, I guess they could have unplugged the cord."

The pickup stopped and Wade rolled down his window. "Trouble?"

Calen opened the car door and stepped out. There was no sense in upsetting Amy with all of this. Wade took the hint and stepped out of his vehicle as well.

"What's up?" Wade said when they were at the back of his pickup.

"Someone's been in your mother's house," Calen said. "They hung a doll from that light over the kitchen table. The rope was around the thing's neck."

Wade drew in his breath. "Whoa. That's nasty."

Calen nodded. "I don't want to get people in a panic, but I think we should make sure the house is clear before we take the women inside. We need to let the sheriff know, too."

Wade reached in his pocket and drew out a small cell phone. "Sometimes we can get service around here and sometimes not."

He opened the phone and turned it on.

Wade nodded to Calen. "Looks like today's a good day for reception." With that, the younger man punched in some numbers. "We'll see if the sheriff answers or not."

The wind was blowing some, and Calen turned around to look in the direction of the ranch house. The clouds in the sky were darker than they had been. Only the barn and the roof of the house were visible from this angle, but he studied them anyway. Even if someone was convinced Gracie had murdered her husband, what would they gain by frightening her? She had already served the jail time for the crime. Everyone knew about the abuse in their family.

A cold drop of rain fell on Calen's nose.

"Yeah, Sheriff Wall," Wade said into the phone. Calen turned around to see that the younger man had cupped his hands around the phone's mouthpiece so he could be heard better. "We have a problem out at the Stone ranch."

Wade didn't say much more than that, but when he was finished he looked back at Calen.

"Why don't you bring Mom and the girl

over to my house? They can stay with Amy while we check out what's gone on."

Calen nodded. "That's probably for the best."

Gracie wouldn't like it, Calen knew that much. But she would do it because she wanted Tessie to be safe.

"I'll make a call to the bunkhouse, too," Calen said then. "In case we need to search the coulee and the fields."

Wade handed his cell phone to Calen. "Just punch in the numbers."

Calen placed his call and told the men what was happening. He asked them to check the back fields on the way over as best they could by driving through the equipment paths, and then hike down to the coulee.

It took all of fifteen minutes for the other Stone vehicles to come down the road and stop to hear why everyone was parked at the beginning of the drive into the main house. Once the men all knew what was happening, though, it didn't take long for them to drive over to Wade's place and check his house, before escorting the women and children inside.

"Nobody leaves until we get back," Wade said, as he turned the lock. "When I close this door, it needs to stay closed until one of us comes to get you."

Calen offered to drive them all back to the

house, since his vehicle was the only one that could carry four grown men.

"So Mom is babysitting your granddaughter?" Jake asked before Calen had even started the car.

It was a mild-sounding question, but he heard the challenge. "Tessie seems to like her."

Jake grunted and turned to look at him. "Of course, she likes her. I just don't want to see someone taking advantage of my mother. With the girl's mom being arrested and all, it brings back hard feelings."

"I'm paying her," Calen said, knowing how inadequate that was.

"Enough to make up for someone hanging that doll at her house?" Jake demanded to know.

"He's also taking her to the church's harvest dinner," Tyler added, his voice amused. "As her date. And we don't know who put that doll there."

Jake grunted again, but didn't say anything.

"The dinner was my idea," Tyler said, clearly pleased with himself.

"I'm not surprised at that." Jake scowled at his younger brother.

Calen was almost glad to get to the main house. No matter what they found inside, it was sure to be less tense there than in this car.

All of the Stone boys got out of the car as soon as Calen pulled it to a stop. He hadn't noticed when it had happened, but they each seemed to have a weapon. Tyler had drawn the knife he kept in his boot for rattlesnakes. Jake had a baseball bat. And Wade had a length of rope so tightly wound that Calen had no doubt it could be used as a whip.

"I'll go around to the front," Tyler said as he slipped away from the shelter of the car. He seemed to blend into the side of the house as he made his way around, bending down to avoid showing his form in any of the windows.

Calen figured that was his military training.

"I'll go around the other way," Jake said, as he went over to circle the house from the other side.

"I guess that leaves us with the back door," Wade said, with a look at Calen. "If we run into any trouble, you leave it to me."

"Now, see here, I was handling my share of trouble before you were born." Calen might not be as young as Gracie's sons, but he wasn't ready for the rocking chair yet.

"I know," Wade said with a grin. "But we Stones take care of our own business."

"Well, I—" Calen started and stopped. He'd almost said it was going to be his business before too long if he had anything to say about it. But just because he wanted to take care of Gracie, that didn't mean he'd risk offending her by speaking out of turn. She'd given him no reason to think she was relying on him for anything.

Before he got his thoughts squared away, Wade was starting toward the house, and Calen had no choice but to follow.

From the time they reached the back door until the four of them had searched every closet and hallway in the house, Calen figured not more than ten minutes had passed. They all ended up back in the kitchen, and Jake reached up and untied the doll from the light cord.

"It took some sick person to do this," Jake said as he set the doll on the table without touching it. He reached for the string to untie it from around the doll's neck, but Tyler put up a hand to stop him.

"Leave it," Tyler said as he turned around. "The sheriff will want to see it the way it is."

"I suppose so," Jake agreed as he sat down in one of the chairs.

"Don't get too comfortable," Wade said. "We still need to check out the barn and the lilac bushes."

"I don't think anybody could hide behind

those bushes," Tyler offered with a grim smile. "Not enough leaves."

"My men will be out looking through the fields," Calen reminded them. "So don't worry if you see someone in the distance."

The Stones began with the same searching techniques they had used in the house. The only difference was that they found Rusty tied up in one of the stalls in the barn. He barked a welcome to them and seemed fine. No one knew how someone had gotten the dog in the barn.

Calen took some hope from the fact that the dog was not harmed. Maybe the actions in the house weren't as malicious as he'd thought. At least Gracie would be relieved that her pet was all right. They untied Rusty before Calen got in the car and went over to Wade's house to bring back the women.

The door opened to him on his first knock, and he assured them all that everyone was safe, even Rusty.

"We're not sure what the motive was, but the sheriff is on his way out and we've done all we can," Calen said.

The four women and two girls squeezed into the car, and Calen drove them over to Gracie's house. This time Rusty was in the driveway barking at them and wagging his tail. Calen smiled as Gracie bent down to hug her pet before walking the rest of the way to her back door.

Maybe things weren't as bad as they looked, he thought.

Then he saw the three Stone boys standing on the porch with their arms crossed. They looked suspicious.

It could be no one in the family had a trusting nature, he told himself.

Chapter Eleven

Gracie smelled the oregano in the spaghetti sauce as she walked over to the hook by the refrigerator and pulled down her red-checked apron. She looked through the window and noticed the sky had grown gray outside, so she flipped the switch for the light to go on above the kitchen sink as well. She always made the full seven quarts of sauce that her slow cooker would hold, because the leftover amount was good to freeze.

"I'll just get the noodles going," she said then, as she tied her apron behind her back. She refused to let her sons know her heart was breaking. They probably weren't even aware that they were huddled around her as they had been as young boys, worried about what their father was going to do and not sure what they could do to stop him anyway.

"You can sit in the living room," she finally said to them, as she pulled a big kettle out from her bottom cupboard. "No one is going to burst through the door when we're all in the house."

Gracie put the kettle in the sink and started the water running.

She remembered sending the boys to bed early sometimes if Buck was out drinking. She could cope with anything better if they were safe. Some family patterns just never changed, though, she told herself, as she turned and noticed none of her sons had moved.

"Your wives could use some water to drink," she said then, as she stepped away from the sink and carried the filled kettle to the stove. Her boys all looked over at the doorway to the living room, where the women stood, no more relaxed than their husbands. Angelina had taken charge of Tessie and had the girl right by her side. Cat had her daughter, Lara. Amy just looked worried.

"It's all right," she assured everyone again as she turned the heat on. "We'll be fine."

She would not let a malicious prank destroy the peace she had found in returning to this home with her family, she told herself as she watched her sons go to the cupboard and each take down a glass.

"We can eat in the living room just this once," she said then. "So you can set up the TV trays that I have in the back closet. We'll pretend it's a picnic."

Calen stepped into the kitchen from the porch just then. He had been checking Rusty out for any wounds that might have not been noticed earlier.

Gracie smiled at him. Calen was a protector like her sons. She hadn't really noticed it until now, though. His eyes looked at her with the same attention to detail that he'd no doubt given to Rusty, but she shook her head slightly. Her sons were upset enough, and she had seen the looks Jake had sent Calen's way. Besides, a man paid attention to a woman for many different reasons. It might mean nothing.

Calen glanced at the table then. "We called the sheriff and told him the place was clear so he didn't need to rush right over."

"He'll appreciate being able to drive his family home from church before he comes here." Gracie turned her attention back to the stove.

She wasn't going to look at what was on the table. A white dish towel had been draped over what must be the Kewpie doll Calen had told her about. She wondered if the sheriff could get some kind of a fingerprint from the doll.

She didn't know whether or not it was best to know who her enemy was. She hadn't thought anyone around here still had a problem with her, at least not one this deep-seated, but she was obviously wrong.

Lord, help me to love whoever it is, she prayed then. She supposed if she knew, maybe she could do something to show the person they had nothing to fear from her.

She listened to Calen's footsteps and noted he didn't walk over to the table, either.

The sound of a vehicle driving to the house came through, and Calen opened the kitchen door slightly. "It's my boys from the bunk-house."

"Invite them in for spaghetti," Gracie said. "We've got plenty."

"You're sure?" Calen asked. "They won't expect to be fed. They're probably just stopping to tell me that they've checked out the coulee."

Gracie walked over and opened the freezer part of her refrigerator. "We've got more than enough spaghetti, and I have several loaves of garlic bread. I'll just bring out another one."

By that time, she could hear the sound of boots on the porch.

"Well, they'll be glad to have a home-cooked meal. We still don't have a cook for the bunkhouse, so we sort of take turns throwing something together for a meal."

"I better add some extra vegetables then," Gracie said with a smile at the man. "My experience with my sons' cooking is that they always forget the vegetables. I imagine you and the ranch hands are the same."

Calen chuckled. "Guilty as charged."

He answered the knock at the door and Gracie was surprised how much better the kitchen felt with another four cowboys in it. She would need to remember that no one could steal her peace of mind if she didn't let them.

Calen's ranch hands were pleased with the dinner invitation, and Gracie pulled down more plates. That would make thirteen of them for the meal, fourteen if they counted Tessie, who would probably need a plastic bowl instead of a plate and would have her own high chair.

"Oh, did that woman call here?" one of the ranch hands asked Calen, as they were setting their hats on the bench Gracie kept near the door just for that purpose.

"What woman?" Calen asked, and then looked over at Gracie.

She shook her head. "No one has called here for you."

"Oh, well, she sounded like one of your

church women. All formal and wouldn't say what she wanted," the ranch hand said, and gave a shrug with his shoulders. "I told her you were over at Gracie Stone's ranch with your granddaughter."

Calen winced. "I wish you hadn't mentioned Tessie."

"They're bound to find out about her soon anyway," Gracie said, as she went to the refrigerator and pulled out several trays of ice cubes. She was tired of having to think about what she said to people. "There aren't any secrets around here that stay that way for long."

"I suppose not," Calen said as he walked over to the stove. "Can I stir something for you?"

"I don't even have the noodles in yet," Gracie said as she looked up in surprise. "It's just boiling water."

"Well, if it needs stirring, I'm your man for it," Calen said as he stepped away. "In the meantime, maybe I can get the ice ready to put in the glasses."

"Now, that would be helpful," Gracie agreed as she opened the box of noodles. "And reach up in the cupboard and bring down those big red napkins. We'll use them, too."

Gracie emptied the noodles into the boiling water. "It won't be long now."

* * *

Twenty minutes later, Calen was sitting on the sofa in Gracie's living room, thinking they should eat in there more often. It had started to rain outside and the sound of the drops on the roof had turned the whole house cozy, especially after the lamps were turned on. Gracie herself was nestled right next to him, and Calen couldn't remember ever sitting that close to someone at a table.

"That was the best spaghetti I've ever eaten," Calen said as he set his plate on the TV tray that he shared with Gracie. He added his napkin to the plate.

Murmurs of agreement could be heard around the room. Between the Stone families and the ranch hands, there were twelve adults scattered around. Jake's daughter, Lara, was sitting on his lap. Gracie had put Tessie's high chair in the doorway to the kitchen, far enough away that anything she dropped or threw would likely land on linoleum instead of carpet.

"The garlic bread is good, too," one of the ranch hands said as he put his last bite in his mouth with relish.

"The best ever," one of the other hands agreed.

Gracie smiled. "I notice no one complimented me on the frozen peas."

"Oh, they were good, too," Calen said, stretching out his legs. "I would have had seconds if I hadn't taken more of that spaghetti."

"Sure," Gracie nodded. "I know how that goes."

Calen was going to say something poetic about the bread, the spaghetti and the peace of the day when he heard a sound that caused him to turn toward the window. "Someone's coming."

All thoughts of poetry fled.

"Probably just Sheriff Wall," Wade said, as he stood from where he had been sitting in the old brown recliner that had belonged to Buck. That chair still meant something to Gracie's boys, and Calen noticed they had all eyed it with some kind of unease as they'd walked by earlier. It had fallen to Wade, as the eldest, to sit in it, since every place in the room was needed today. Calen had a hunch the chair wasn't used often, though.

"Likely is the sheriff," Calen agreed, but he stood up, too, just in case.

He had heard the engine in the sheriff's car enough in the last couple of days that he thought he should recognize it. The car coming in sounded like it was a lighter-weight vehicle, though. Maybe a four-cylinder car instead of six. That's when he heard the second engine farther away. Now, that was the sheriff's car.

He couldn't picture Mary or one of the other Sunday-school teachers making the drive out here to talk to either Gracie or him, but stranger things had happened on this day. He looked down at Gracie. He didn't have the heart to share his worries with her. But he didn't want her caught unaware, either. He knew how she hated that.

"Know anyone with a small car?" Calen asked as he started over to the window.

"No," Gracie said. "No one comes here but us."

With all of the legs to step over, Calen didn't make it to the window behind the sofa in time to see the car. It had already driven to the other side of the house by then. He did see the sheriff's car coming over the rise, though.

"Well, I expect whoever it is, it's nothing to worry about." Calen stepped back from the window. "Most people should be home with their families today anyway."

Calen expected the knock at the kitchen door and was halfway through the living room when he heard it. "I'll get it."

He glanced back, nodding at Gracie so she would sit back down and relax.

If it was someone from the church, Calen

planned to take a message and tell them that Gracie would contact them later. It was the Lord's Day, after all.

Calen opened the door.

"Hello?" He didn't recognize the middle-aged woman standing there. She had sandy hair, cut in a smooth line to match her chin. She wore glasses, but he could see her mossy-green eyes were alert and intelligent. She wore a beige suit and only a small amount of makeup.

"Calen Gray?" she asked.

He frowned slightly. No one wore a suit around here if they didn't have to. He let his eyes travel lower and that was when he saw the briefcase.

"I'm sorry, I— Yes, I'm Calen," he finally said.

Lord, have mercy on me, he started to pray.

"I'm Mrs. Schneider," the woman said as she held out her hand. "From the Montana Family Services Department. I've come to see you about Tessie Hampton. May I come in?"

The woman's voice was not loud, but Calen heard the silence that came over the whole house.

Calen took the woman's hand and shook it as long as he dared. "Of course."

He stepped to the side.

"I can explain," he said when she was inside the kitchen. "I love Tessie. She's my grand-daughter, but—"

"This must be Tessie," the woman said, her voice more pleasant than he had expected.

Calen had no choice but to turn around.

"My, you must like spaghetti," the woman said as she walked over to the high chair.

Tessie sat there, red sauce in her hair, on her chin, her elbow, the floor and likely the bottoms of her shoes. She even had a fistful of noodles in her hand.

"We give her other food, too," Calen said as he walked over to the sink and dampened a paper towel. They couldn't deny him tem-porary custody because of her table manners, could they? "I plan to get some fruit tomor-row. The stores are closed today."

He was talking too much and he knew it. But what was the family-services lady think-ing—to surprise a man like this.

"It's Sunday, you know," he said, which seemed to sum up the only excuse he had.

Fortunately, Gracie had come to the door-way.

"We just got back from church and are hav-ing a family dinner," Gracie said with a stiff smile.

Now, why hadn't he thought of that, Calen

asked himself. "Gracie and I even taught the weekly Sunday-school class for Tessie—and her friends."

It was a stretch, Calen knew, to say they were friends, but his granddaughter had played very nicely with the other children. That should give them all points, shouldn't it? And they would have to be impressed that he and Gracie had taught that class. The woman didn't need to know that the regular teacher was desperate for a substitute.

There was another knock and Calen turned around and looked. The sheriff stood in the open doorway.

"You need to start locking up around here," Sheriff Wall said as he stepped inside the kitchen.

Calen's heart sank. This couldn't be good.

"Sheriff, have you met Mrs. Schneider?" Calen figured the sheriff would be smart enough to be discreet, given the circumstances.

"I gave her directions to find you," the lawman said as he tipped his hat in the general direction of the woman. "Glad to see you made it."

"I only had trouble at the first turn," the state woman said with an answering nod. "Thank you."

They were all silent for a minute at that betrayal from Sheriff Wall. Calen was unsure if he should say more. Gracie looked poised to grab Tessie and run. Even the family-services woman seemed at a little bit of a loss as to what to say next.

"Well, don't let me get in the way," the sheriff finally said, as he walked over to the table and pulled a pair of plastic gloves out of his pocket. "I take it that this is what you have for me?"

With that, the sheriff put the gloves on and pulled the dish towel back. The Kewpie doll was revealed, lying on its back with its chubby arms in the air. The noose was still around its neck, and its yellow braid was spread to one side on the table. The faded red-gingham shirt was the only cheerful thing about the toy.

Calen held his breath, hoping the family-services woman wouldn't ask about the doll. No one would let a child stay in a house that was being terrorized by some unknown person.

The sheriff held up the doll to look at it more closely.

"Dolly!" The shriek was coming from Tessie's mouth with more force than she'd said any word in all her time around them. She dropped the noodles she'd been holding and reached out her hands. "Dolly! Mine!"

"Oh." Calen's heart almost stopped. He looked at Gracie. She was stunned. Then he looked back to the sheriff. The lawman stood there with his mouth hanging open.

Only the family-services woman seemed to have her wits about her. She walked closer to the table and frowned. "What's that noose doing around the neck of Tessie's dolly?"

"I—it—" Calen saw his whole future pass before his eyes, and it wasn't good. "It's not what it looks like."

The woman turned around, her eyes icy cold. "What possible reason could anyone have for doing this to that poor child?"

"But we didn't," Calen protested. "I mean, someone did, yes. But not me. Not Gracie."

The woman looked him over. "Gracie is the one who is taking care of the child, as I understand it?"

Calen nodded. "Just until Tessie can get used to me. She's a little nervous around men."

"Humph," the woman said. Calen wasn't sure what to make of that, other than it sounded like she sympathized with Tessie on that one.

"I can vouch for Calen and Gracie both," Sheriff Wall said. "And they sure didn't do anything to this doll."

"That's right," Calen said. "We've never even seen that doll before this."

He glanced over at Gracie. She shook her head.

"No," he repeated. "We've never seen it."

And that, he realized, was perhaps the most troubling thing that had happened today.

"It wasn't in Tessie's suitcase," Gracie said. "That's sitting in my bedroom and I've gone through it several times."

"It wasn't in the car trunk," Tyler added. "I popped the trunk and gave the car a good look over yesterday, before you got back from the hospital."

"Well, that just doesn't make any sense," the sheriff said as he scratched his head.

Calen almost hoped the doll was some senseless thing, because it sure beat the suspicion that was growing in his mind.

Gracie looked at him and he knew she suspected it, too.

"It could be Carter Benson," Calen said, his voice low. He would be happy if he was proven wrong.

Gracie bent down so she was on eye level with Tessie. "Sweetie, did someone take your dolly?"

Tessie nodded vigorously. "Bad man."

The room was silent for a full minute.

"Well," the sheriff said finally. "That sure changes things." He was quiet for a bit longer. "He was sending a message to Renee. If she says she made up the story about him being with them, he gets off. Everyone would stop looking for him. He'd be home free."

"I don't see how he would figure Renee would get the message," Wade said.

The sheriff shrugged. "We didn't make a big deal at the hospital about taking Renee to the jail. Everyone knows she left, but we made it look like she was just checking out. Maybe he thinks she would come back here. Her car's here."

"No one is spending another night in this house until we find this man," Tyler said then. "We have more than enough room at our place. And we'll put on the security system."

"But—" Gracie started.

"Rusty will come, too," Tyler said. "If he can stay inside here at night, another night or two inside at our place won't hurt him."

"So, let me get this straight," Mrs. Schneider said as she looked from one to the other of the people there. "Tessie is in danger?"

"Not as long as I have breath in my body," Calen vowed.

"She'll be fine with this crew," the sheriff said as he waved an arm around to indicate everyone. "Tyler's not kidding about that security system he has. State of the art. Bulletproof glass on the windows. Locks that can't be picked. The works."

Mrs. Schneider hesitated. "Well, I don't really have a place for her. And I wouldn't want to surprise someone on Sunday afternoon."

Calen bit his tongue until he could say, "Thank you."

The sheriff reached into his pocket and pulled out a large plastic bag. He picked the Kewpie doll up and slipped it inside.

"Dolly?" Tessie said, her voice quiet this time but no less heartrending.

"I'm sorry, sweetie," Gracie said as she patted Tessie on her arm.

Calen remembered something he had done when Renee was about Tessie's age. He reached into his suit pocket and pulled out a pristine white handkerchief, the one he kept with his suit. He made a few cowboy knots in the thing until it had a head and a flowing skirt.

He walked over and presented it to Tessie with a courtly bow. He set it on the tray of the high chair, and the figure looked like a lady in white.

"Dolly," Tessie said in delight as she picked it up. She waved the thing around, making her dolly dance for her. Then she looked right at Calen and smiled.

His heart melted.

"Well," Mrs. Schneider said as she looked at him, too, with more tolerance in her eyes than she'd shown thus far. "That's nice."

"Thank you," Calen said. Maybe his granddaughter would let him hold her sometime, after all.

Everyone watched Tessie play with her dancing doll for a few moments.

"I guess we better get the dishes washed," Gracie said then.

"Mom," Tyler protested. "We need to get everyone somewhere safe. We don't have time for the dishes."

Gracie drew herself up and stood straight. "If someone is going to break into my house, they are going to find my dishes are done and the beds are made."

Tyler just shook his head.

"You folks just be sure and lock the doors when you leave," the sheriff said as he turned with the Kewpie doll in his hand. "I want to get this to the lab boys as fast as I can. I have a man that I can have patrol around here tonight just in case this Carter fellow comes back. In the meantime, I want to see if his fingerprints match any we have in the system. That likely is not his real name, and the prints will tell us who he is."

The sheriff turned to the door.

Wade stepped into the kitchen then. He'd gathered up some of the plates. "I'll get to washing. You go pack what you need for the night, Mom."

Gracie nodded and took a step toward the bedroom, but then she turned around and looked right at Calen. "But where will you be?"

"At the bunkhouse. I don't want to put Tyler out any."

"Don't worry about it," Tyler said. "We've got plenty of room for you if you can spare some time to stay. It'd be nice to have another man in the house for a change."

Calen nodded. "I would sleep better knowing everyone's okay."

"It's settled then," Tyler said.

Gracie turned around then to continue on to her bedroom. Calen was glad, because that meant she didn't see the victory sign Tyler flashed his brothers. Wade grinned, but Jake scowled something fierce.

Calen pretended he didn't see anything. He was coming to realize those boys might be touchy about having a new man pay attention to their mother, even if he was only a friend.

Then he looked through to the living room at that old brown recliner. It wouldn't hurt those boys to have a few things change around the ranch anyway. He must have stood there staring for a few minutes, because when he turned around, the sheriff and the family-services woman were both walking out the door.

The two officials called their goodbyes from the edge of the porch.

Calen called his thanks back to them.

Then he walked over to the table and picked up the dish towel that had been covering the Kewpie doll. He folded it and set it on the counter by the refrigerator. Gracie would like everything neat when they left.

He looked over at Tessie then. He figured neat might take a while when it came to his granddaughter, though. Not that he cared how messy she was as long as he could keep her safe.

Chapter Twelve

It was ten o'clock Thursday morning and Gracie was sitting inside the fortress of the house her son Tyler had built at his father-in-law's direction. She hoped she was never cursed with that much money. Not a bit of natural sunlight made it through the tinted, bulletproof windows or the airtight metal doors. Maybe if they didn't have the security system on, it would be different, as they could open the windows to let in the outside world without setting off alarms in three different counties.

But, in the meantime, she sat here in the temperature-controlled living room with its white marble fireplace and white crystal lamps. If it wasn't for Tessie sitting on her lap, Gracie would have been bored senseless in the past two days. And the toddler was only supposed to be with her for ten minutes at a time. Her daughters-in-law had said they didn't want Gracie to be stressed with too much child care, and they would be coming for the girl in a minute or two. She didn't know what had happened to make her sons' wives think she couldn't take care of a child.

"At least your grandpa gets to go to the ranch and work," Gracie said, bending down to whisper to the toddler. "I wonder what he's doing right now?"

Gracie figured things had gotten pretty low in her life when all she could think about was what Calen Gray was doing. Not that she'd ask him when he came back late tonight. She didn't want him to think she was nosy. Or interested. Besides, it was only because she was so bored that she even wondered about it. She would be giving the same thought to Rusty's whereabouts if the dog wasn't in the house at her feet most of the day.

"We're all growing soft," Gracie complained to the girl in her lap, who didn't seem to care as long as she could chew on the handle of the plastic mirror her grandfather had given her to play with before he'd left this morning.

Gracie looked down at Rusty. "You know what I mean, don't you, old fella?"

The dog yawned.

At least it wouldn't be too long before her surprise, Gracie thought as she glanced over at the gold-framed white clock on the fireplace mantel. She had to squint to be able to read the gold numbers, but she figured only eight minutes had passed since she'd checked it last. When she'd said something to her daughters-in-law earlier about how slow time was moving, they had looked at her, grinned and said that would soon change.

Gracie rubbed the back of her neck to ease a bit of stiffness she'd gotten there lately. She couldn't imagine what her sons' wives could be planning, but she had to admit she hadn't been the most patient of guests in the last couple of days. She missed her own bed. She missed the light coming through the kitchen windows. She missed her home.

But she liked the excitement she saw on the faces of her sons' wives. Maybe they were planning a cookout on the fancy barbecue grill Tyler and Angelina had on their patio. That sounded good to Gracie and it would be lunchtime soon enough. She promised herself she would look surprised when they led her out there.

There was nothing worse, in her opinion, than a spoilsport who couldn't enjoy a good surprise. Everyone was entitled to see the targeted person's face light up in delight after all the work they'd done to plan everything.

"I wonder if they'll grill any shrimp," Gracie muttered dreamily as she looked down at Rusty. "Angelina knows I like shrimp, and her father ships it to her by the case."

The dog perked up at the mention of the seafood. And he didn't even know she'd spied a large wooden crate yesterday sitting by the freezer. It was empty, of course, but the freezer was extra-large and had plenty of room for a case of shrimp.

"I guess there are some advantages to all that money," Gracie conceded. Maybe it wouldn't be so bad to be rich. Especially when one considered that Angelina's father had used part of the money to try some new treatments for his cancer and was alive today because of his wealth. He was determined to be around to see his grandchild born.

Gracie settled deeper into the chair, figuring she would relax before lunch.

She must have dozed then, because she woke up with a start when she heard the sound of laughter coming from the kitchen. She looked down at her lap and noticed it was empty. Someone had come to get Tessie. Even Rusty was gone.

"Now, ladies," Gracie heard a familiar voice say with authority.

Gracie smiled. It would be no trouble to be delighted about this surprise. It sounded as though the girls had invited Mrs. Hargrove to join them for lunch. The older woman was one of Gracie's favorite people, and the fact that she was here meant she'd recovered from that horrible flu she'd had on Sunday.

Mrs. Hargrove wasn't too fond of shrimp, though, so maybe they'd be grilling hamburgers, after all.

"But that's okay," Gracie said as she stood and smoothed down her blouse. "I'll take the company instead of the shrimp, especially today."

She walked to the hallway that led to the kitchen and then stopped. She didn't want to walk in on her surprise and spoil anything. Maybe she should go back in the living room and make some noise so they'd know she was awake.

Gracie tiptoed back down the hall and then looked around the living room. The problem with all the plush whiteness was that there was hardly any way to make noise if she wanted to. Fortunately, she didn't have to wait long, because someone opened the door at the other end of the hall.

She turned around to see it was Amy.

"Oh, hi," Gracie said as she gave an elaborate stretch, pretending she'd just awakened. She hadn't counted on the stiffness in her shoulders, but that didn't stop her. "I was coming out to get something to drink."

Amy grinned. "Good, because I was just coming to get you. I knew you wouldn't want to miss out on one minute of this, not when you're going stir-crazy being inside all day."

Gracie nodded and tried to not look smug. "So we're going outside?"

What else could it be but a patio party? She congratulated herself on her guess as she walked down the hall toward Amy.

"Well, no," Amy said as she turned around. She had the sweetest face and now she looked worried. "We need to stay inside. The sheriff told us that much. You haven't tried to sneak out, have you?"

Gracie shook her head. Okay, so it wasn't the patio. But she figured the shrimp would still taste good even if it was done on the indoor grill that Angelina had built into her kitchen.

"I just hope no one went to much trouble," Gracie added.

Amy shook her head and then stopped to think. "Well, I guess it is some trouble, but

Angelina has that big counter in the kitchen and it's the perfect place to cut things up."

Gracie didn't bother to hide her grin, since Amy was facing away from her anyway.

Gracie figured it must mean shrimp ka-bobs. Maybe some green peppers and mush-rooms along with the shrimp. She wouldn't mind some of those little onions on the skewer either.

Amy pushed open the door to the kitchen and stepped through.

By the time Gracie got to the door, she was starting to wonder why she didn't smell anything cooking. In fact, she sniffed the air again; it smelled like glue.

She went through the door even though she was beginning to think she actually was going to be surprised.

"Oh." Gracie's smile froze on her face.

There were women all over the kitchen. By the table. By the counter. Opening the refrig-erator. And when she looked close, she rec-ognized them.

Her daughter-in-law, Cat, cleared her throat.

"Calen said you had mentioned wanting to help with the decorations for the harvest din-ner," Cat said from where she stood, at the end of the counter with a pair of scissors in her hands. On the counter beneath her were sheets of yellow tissue paper, some of it already cut into circles.

Gracie told herself the circles were good. But when she let her eyes wander over the kitchen again, she did not know if she could hide her dismay. All of the young mothers from the church were sitting in chairs at the tables, scissors and tissue paper in front of them just as it was with Cat.

They were clearly making fall flowers. Golden, rust and burgundy colors. Even some dark cream and brown flowers. She saw a few deep purple ones. The jumble of tissue paper covered every surface in the kitchen and threatened to cascade over to the floor.

She heard the sound of children giggling off to the side in the play area that Tyler and Angelina had already set up for their unborn child. It sounded like a teenage girl was supervising in there.

Gracie was trying to focus, but it wasn't working. She did need to get her eyes examined, she thought as she blinked a few times. Everything about her was aching.

"You don't look so good." A voice cut through her blur, and Gracie turned to see Mrs. Hargrove walking toward her, with purpose in her steps. The older woman's gray hair was pulled back into a bun and she was wearing a green-and-white gingham housedress with a starched white apron. Her dear face was frowning in concern at Gracie.

"I'm fine." Gracie forced herself to smile. She could see her daughters-in-law all looking at her with worried looks on their faces, too. This is not what she had planned. "I don't want to be a spoilsport."

"Nonsense," Mrs. Hargrove said as she walked closer and put her hand on Gracie's forehead. "You look the way I did when I was coming down with the flu."

"I can't be getting the flu," Gracie protested. "I had the flu shot."

Mrs. Hargrove stepped back slightly and took a long look at Gracie. "Have you been tired lately?"

"Well, yes, but—"

"Do your joints ache? Your elbows? Your fingers?" Mrs. Hargrove demanded to know. "Even your eyeballs?"

"I guess so," Gracie admitted. "But I don't think that means I have the flu. At my age, I get achy and tired."

"Only when you're coming down with the flu," Mrs. Hargrove said in a tone that declared the matter was settled in her mind. "Besides, the flu shot doesn't prevent every kind of flu. I never should have sent you into that

Sunday-school class. Half of those kids are down with the flu by now."

"Let me get your some juice." A voice penetrated Gracie's mind and she looked over at Amy, who had been the one to speak.

"No," Gracie gasped. Maybe she was sick. "I don't want you to get anything. Think of the baby. Think of those poor, sweet children in Mrs. Hargrove's class."

"It's all right, dear," the Sunday-school teacher, Mary, said as she stepped close to Amy. "I'll get it for her."

Then Mary turned to Gracie and said, "You just go lie down on the sofa. And don't you worry about the children. They're all doing fine. I'll bring you some juice and crackers. Or would you like tea? I know you always drink tea at church."

Did everyone watch what she drank, Gracie wondered? She was glad she'd thrown away that old juice bottle.

"And try not to worry," the older woman continued with a smile. "We have lots of experience with this flu. You'll be all better in twenty-four hours. Just in time to go to the harvest dinner and watch the children put on their skit."

"Good," Gracie managed. "Tea would be nice."

"I know your Mr. Gray will be glad, too.

The two of you will have a fine date. I've already put it on the prayer chain."

Could her life get any worse? Gracie wondered.

Just then the doorbell rang. Which triggered the automatic-dog barking, since the security system was on high alert. The dog barking had been Angelina's idea. She thought it was cute. But now, Rusty started to bark in support of the electronic dogs, and Gracie decided maybe she should go lie down on the sofa, after all. The more she thought about it, the more her eyeballs did hurt.

Calen stepped into the kitchen of Tyler's house just in time to see Gracie walking down the hall to the living room. Thankfully, someone had turned the barking alarm off. Her shoulders were slumped and she walked as if her bones ached. Then he looked around at the women and the tissue paper, and his heart sank.

"What's happening?" he asked more calmly than he felt.

Calen thought the sheriff was supposed to have men guarding the house so no one could come in unexpectedly. Even at that, someone needed to shut down the security system for a few minutes, at least. He had a special pass, but who had let all these women in here?

"Mom has been kind of down," Amy answered as she looked at him. "And you had said she indicated she wanted to help decorate for the harvest dinner."

"I did say that," Calen admitted, wishing he had left well enough alone.

He'd never expected there to be anything like this, though. He was just trying to make the point that Gracie had good community spirit even though she had refused to teach Sunday school again, something that had seemed to distress her pregnant daughters-in-law. They seemed to think she might not be anxious to have more little children around, and he was simply trying to help them see that Gracie was a vital part of things around here and her decision about the Sunday-school class meant nothing.

"Well, we couldn't go to the church to help," Amy explained as she set her scissors down on a pile of yellow tissue circles. "So we thought we'd invite everyone to come here to work."

Calen nodded. He got the picture.

"We didn't know Mom was coming down with the flu," Amy continued.

"She is?" Calen asked.

Not that he doubted Gracie felt something, but it did seem a little too convenient.

"I'll go check on her," he said.

Then Mary smiled up at him. She was holding a tray with a cup of tea on it and some crackers. He also saw she'd added a little pitcher of cream and some sugar cubes.

"I'm just taking this in to her," the older woman said. "Would you like a cup of tea, too?"

"I'm fine." Calen smiled his thanks. "In fact, I can carry the tray in for you, if you'd like. No sense in you getting exposed to the flu."

"Ohhh." The woman trilled a little laugh. "I suppose you do want to see your sweetheart."

"Oh." Calen had to blink at that.

"We've all heard about your date for the harvest festival," the woman leaned close and whispered.

Why she bothered to keep her voice low, Calen didn't know. Not when he could tell by the looks in everyone's eyes that they already knew.

"Did Gracie tell you that?" Calen had asked.

"Oh, no," the older woman said. "Tyler told us. Well, he didn't tell us, really, but we heard him arguing with his brother Jake over the telephone, and he happened to mention it. He had to let us through the security system, since there were so many of us. We would have triggered the riot response, he said. Have you ever seen a house like this?"

Calen had to shake his head. He wasn't sure he ever wanted to see another house like this one, either. But he couldn't say that, not when Mary was looking at him with such bright eyes.

"It is a wonder, isn't it?" he finally said as he lifted the tray from her hands. He looked at the tea and the crackers. "I don't suppose anyone has some aspirin, too?"

Several hands reached for purses, but Amy held out a bottle first. She'd had it in her apron pocket.

"It's not for me," she said as she set the bottle on the tray. "I keep it for Wade."

Calen nodded. That was the first sensible thing he'd heard since he'd stepped into the house. He'd come to notice that Wade had a tough role in the Stone family. He was the oldest son and his brothers Jake and Tyler both looked to him for advice and guidance. They still missed having had a father in their teenage years and probably didn't even know it. The only reason he knew was that he'd seen the same thing in half the young men who worked for him at the Elkton Ranch.

Calen balanced the tray in his hands and began his walk into Tyler's white living room.

He saw Gracie huddled up on the sofa.

"Heard you were sick," he said, as he set the tray down on the glass-and-gold coffee table by the sofa.

Gracie turned when she saw it was him. If he wasn't mistaken, she looked healthier than she had before she'd known it was him.

"I don't know if I'm sick or not," she admitted. "But I didn't think I should take any chances."

Calen chuckled. "Just what I figured, too. Want me to put some cream in your tea?"

"Please," she said as she looked at the tray. "We could get another cup if you want some, too."

Calen added the cream to her tea and held it out to her. "Never could stand tea."

"Really?" Gracie asked, her eyebrows lifting as she took the cup he offered. "But I always thought...I mean, you've drunk—how much tea at my house?"

"Gallons," Calen admitted as he sat down on the chair next to her. "But I figure it's time to be honest. I don't like the stuff."

"Okay," Gracie said as she took a long sip. "I hope you don't mind if I enjoy it."

"I'm happy you do," Calen said as he clasped his hands together.

They were silent for a moment.

"Mind if I ask if you ever got a marker for Buck's grave?" Calen finally asked. "I know you talked about ordering one early on, but wasn't sure if you ever followed through."

Gracie shook her head. "I just didn't seem to get it done."

He let her drink some more tea, hoping he wasn't going to upset her.

"Any reason you keep that old chair of his in your living room?" he finally asked. "The brown recliner Buck used to sit in."

"It's a perfectly good chair," Gracie said.

"The boys hate it," he said. "Brings back bad memories. If it's still a good chair, give it away to someone who never knew Buck."

Calen held his breath. He didn't know if Gracie had any idea what he was asking of her, but he thought she might. Buck had been dead for a long time, but he still lived in that house with her. Until she got the man out of there, she wouldn't be free.

He was relieved when she slowly nodded her head.

"Would you help?" she asked. "I'll find someone to take the chair, if you'll help move it to wherever they live."

"I'd like that," Calen said.

They had a chance, he told himself. He

didn't know if it was enough. But it was more than they'd had yesterday.

"Want a cracker?" Gracie offered with a wave of her hand toward the tray.

"Don't mind if I do," Calen said as he reached for one.

They sat in silence, eating, for a few minutes.

"Did you ask the sheriff about Renee?" Gracie said then.

Calen nodded. "He still thinks she's safest where she is until they find that Carter fellow. But then we're going to go for bail. I found a lawyer to help us and everything."

"Well, then I hope the man comes snooping around here again," Gracie said. "He'll be coming right into a trap."

Gracie never lacked for courage, Calen thought proudly. And then he remembered the young women from the church, sitting out in the kitchen now. He guessed she did waver in her bravery sometimes. But then, he told himself, she could be excused, since she was sick.

"We'll be ready for him," Calen said. He hoped he was speaking the truth.

Chapter Thirteen

Friday morning Gracie went into the house she'd called home for more than twenty years and entered her bedroom. Tyler had made arrangements with the sheriff's guard who was stationed there so she could look through her closet and find something to wear for the harvest dinner tonight. Cat was babysitting Tessie, and it was the first time Gracie had been truly alone in several days. She sat down on the corner of the bed, expecting to be relieved just to sit in her room again, surrounded by these familiar things.

But the sense of belonging didn't come to her.

She looked around more closely then, wondering why it hadn't. Sunlight was filtering through the lace curtains that she'd hung on the window the day she had come here as a bride. She remembered how romantic they had seemed to her back then. Mrs. Hargrove had packed them away when Gracie had been sent to prison. She'd been so busy since she'd come back that she hadn't really looked at them until now. For some reason, they seemed a little ragged, as though they'd been washed too many times and lost any starch they'd ever had.

Gracie turned to get a better view of her entire bedroom. She'd painted the room when she'd come back, but she'd kept the same bland color, neither beige nor white but something in between. The picture on the wall, at the head of their bed, was one Buck had picked out because he'd liked the brilliant orange poppies in the foreground. She hated orange. The quilt on the bench under the window was one his mother had made for their wedding present. There were many shades of orange in that too, and it was one of the first things Gracie saw every morning when she woke up.

She looked around again, this time in bewilderment. She wondered who she was in this room and why it had taken her so long to see she wasn't represented here. Buck had always been so opinionated that there had been no place for her likes or dislikes. She'd never felt like a doormat when she'd been married, but maybe she had compromised too often. Going against her husband's opinions seemed like pushing at a boulder that would never move. Maybe she'd given up because it was just too much work to have a voice.

She stood up and walked across the room to look in the mirror hanging on her closet door. Even the way she wore her hair was something Buck had chosen. When he was alive, she had been happy enough to wear her hair long and braided the way he'd wanted. It seemed a small thing. And then, when she'd gone to prison, the style of her hair was the least of her concerns.

She lifted her hair now, wondering if some fullness around her face would make her look younger, more feminine.

The sound of boots walking across the kitchen linoleum drew her out of her thoughts.

"Mom," Tyler said even before he reached her room.

"I'm here," she answered.

"I got the stuff we needed from the barn," her son said as he stood in the open doorway. "Need some help?"

Gracie smiled. "I think I can manage."

She knew her clothes well; she didn't have that many of them. She pushed back the closet door and reached for two hangers.

"I've got this one," Gracie said as she held up the black dress she'd worn for the reporter on Sunday. "It's got classic lines and goes anywhere."

"What else?" Tyler demanded to know.

Gracie brought out the navy dress she'd purchased right after she was released from prison. She had thought she might need to look for a job back then, before her sons had started returning home to work the ranch with her. "This one is good quality. A little plain, but not bad."

Tyler had a slight frown on his face as he crossed the room to look into the closet for himself.

"I guess I could wear a nice blouse and some pants," Gracie said. "That's always comfortable and—"

"What about this?" Tyler emerged from the back of the closet holding a deep rose satin dress with a scooped neckline and no sleeves. A clear plastic bag covered the outfit. Another sign of Mrs. Hargrove's packing.

"But I got that in high school." Gracie shook her head. "I was going to wear it to the senior prom, and then Buck and I had a fight."

She'd babysat for months to pay for that dress.

"At least there's some color to it. And your size hasn't changed."

"But its floor-length," Gracie protested again. He might not have noticed that because of the plastic bag. "I'm not going to the harvest dinner wearing something that formal."

The women in the church would really have something to talk about then, she thought. They'd say she was putting on airs, trying to pretend she was going somewhere fancy like the opera. Everyone knew the harvest dinner was a simple potluck. No linen napkins or crystal goblets. Mrs. Hargrove's housedresses would be more at home there than what Tyler still held in his hand.

"The dress has a strip of glitter, too," she told her son in case he couldn't see that under the plastic. "It's more like Las Vegas than Dry Creek."

Tyler looked undeterred as he stood there. All of her boys had inherited some of their father's stubbornness.

"I know you want me to make a good impression on Calen," Gracie finally said patiently. She might as well address the real issue. "And I appreciate that. But we—well, it's just not going to work between him and me like you think."

She had her son's attention then.

"Like I think, huh?" Tyler smiled. "What's to think? He's a good man."

"I know, but we're just friends."

If she was going to avoid what had happened in her marriage with Buck, she might as well start now. She didn't ever want to live in a man's shadow again.

Tyler grinned. "I was just friends with Angelina. Jake was just friends with Cat. Even Wade was just friends with Amy. I'd say the Stone family has the just-friends area pretty well covered."

"It's different for all of you, and you know it," Gracie said in exasperation.

Tyler laughed at that, but he kept the rose dress in his hand while he stepped into the middle of the room. "This one still has my vote. Cat knows how to sew, and she can hem up the length and get rid of the strip of glitter if that's what you want."

Gracie almost insisted on taking the navy one instead, but she looked around her bedroom. Maybe it was time she tried something new even if she didn't want a man in her life. And she always had wanted to wear that dress. It had color and life and just felt like the young woman she'd been before everything had happened.

"Would you mind if I stayed with you for a few extra days?" Gracie asked impulsively. "After they catch that guy, Carter? I'd like to have the bedroom painted. Maybe in a deep rose like the dress. And new curtains, bedspread. The works. I'll be so glad to get rid of that awful orange."

Tyler chuckled, but then he walked over to kiss her on the forehead.

"Of course," he said gently.

Gracie had moved close to the dresser and she reached over to open her jewelry box. "I think I'll wear that white strand of pearls you boys got me with the dress, too."

"Mom, those are nothing. We got them at the secondhand store in Miles City. They have to be imitation."

"They're precious to me." She drew them out of the box. They'd saved their allowance for three months to buy them for her birthday one year.

"We should get you some real pearls," Tyler said as he looked at the necklace she held. "Those things have seen better days."

"So have I," Gracie said, smiling as she slipped them into her pocket.

She followed Tyler out of the room and closed the door behind them both.

"Maybe we should paint the living room while we're at it," Tyler said as he walked into the room and stopped to look around.

Gracie nodded and took a breath. "We might even get rid of Dad's old chair."

Tyler grunted. "Now, that would be a blessing."

Gracie didn't say anything. Calen had been right about her boys not wanting the reminder of their father. She couldn't blame them. Buck had started out as an indifferent father and only gotten worse over time.

"Do you ever miss your father?" she asked her youngest son. She couldn't remember asking him that before, and he'd been the one to want a relationship with Buck more than the other two boys.

Tyler was silent for a few minutes. He didn't move.

"I miss a lot of things," he finally said. "Mostly, though, I guess I miss the things he never did."

Gracie waited. She knew her son, and there was more.

"I always wished he would have taken me fishing," Tyler finally said, his voice low and quiet. "Just once." He paused for a bit and continued. "Like Calen used to do. It was nice— a boy and a man sitting there talking about things they might do someday, or questions they had about rattlesnakes or anything that came to mind."

Gracie nodded. "Maybe when we get the painting done inside here, we can order a marker for your father's grave and finally—" She let her voice trail off, and then continued, "Put the poor man to rest."

Tyler didn't move and he didn't say anything.

Then, when he did answer, his voice was low and fierce.

"We don't know what to say on a marker. That's the problem. Or we boys would have done it sooner. We can't agree. Jake wants something funny—like Here Lies the Last of the Hardheaded Stones." Tyler stopped and looked at his mother. "Wade says we should say something like Here Lies Buck Stone, Rancher.' Just that—no mention of him being a husband or a father. Just something to tie him to the land. That's all he cared about anyway."

"That's not true," Gracie started, and then faltered. "He cared about you boys. You should have seen how proud he was when you were all born."

"Even me?" Tyler asked.

Gracie nodded. "Your father just didn't show it."

"That's what Wade always says."

Gracie bowed her head. "I had no idea

you boys had talked about this. The marker and everything."

"We didn't want to trouble you with it."

"I know," Gracie said then, looking at her son. "I'm not complaining. I just—well, I guess it's time, that's all. We need to put the marker on his grave and move on with our lives. We'll think of something to say that is respectable, but not a lie."

"It's not a lie to say we loved him," Tyler said. "At least I did. Sometimes."

Gracie put her hand on her son's arm. "I wish things had been different."

"It could have been worse," Tyler said with a wry smile as he put his hand over hers. "At least we had you for a mother."

With that, they continued to walk out of the house, Tyler with the dress draped over his shoulder and Gracie trying not to let her tears fall when he could see them.

"You know," Tyler said when they reached the kitchen door, "you're going to look good in this dress. Calen is going to be impressed."

Gracie smiled up at her son. "You never give up, do you?"

"Nope," he said as he opened the door to let them step out onto the porch.

Gracie followed him, wondering what her son would do if Calen was impressed with her old prom dress. Her boys might think they wanted her to date someone, but in reality they might not like it. It was foolish to speculate about it all anyway. She had a good life with her sons and their families. It was enough.

Ten hours later, just as the sunset was beginning to spread its rosy color across the sky, Calen parked his borrowed car beside Tyler's fortress of a house and sat there, running his finger under the collar of his new white shirt. He'd just shaved and his hair was squeaky clean. He didn't feel ready, though. If he didn't get out of the sedan soon, however, he figured some alarm was likely to be triggered.

The police in three states hadn't caught sight of that Carter fellow, so the sheriff told everyone they could go back to their normal lives tomorrow. Renee's attorney planned to ask for bail, even if that put her whereabouts on the public record. They couldn't wait forever for the bad guy to show, especially since he could be down in Mexico by now.

Not that Calen was going to spend the evening worrying about all of that.

Instead, he opened his car door and reached over to pick up the pink-rose corsage he'd bought in Miles City a few hours ago. He'd also purchased a new doll, nearly the size of Tessie, which was in the back near the child's seat.

Calen figured the doll would be a success, but he worried about the corsage. He'd told the florist to put on as many rosebuds as she could fit, and it was a generous arrangement. Tyler had assured him that light pink was the right color, but Calen worried that the size of the corsage might make Gracie feel uncomfortable. He knew women generally didn't wear flowers to the harvest dinners at church, but everyone already knew he was taking Gracie there on a date. And, one thing he would say for the people of Dry Creek, they understood that a first date needed to be special. They'd be disappointed if there wasn't something like the corsage to show he was serious.

Knowing that Gracie only had two dresses, the black one and the blue one, he had told himself that this much pink would still not be considered flashy. She'd probably hide it behind one of those big white aprons anyway. Most of the women kept an apron in the church basement, since every kind of meeting meant food was served. They'd have the potluck before the harvest program tonight, so some women would wear their aprons all evening.

Not that he cared who saw the corsage, he

reminded himself as he began the walk to the house. The flowers were for Gracie and no one else. She could keep them in her purse if she felt better about it. He'd always pictured her with dozens of roses in her arms, and all of them from him, but he'd wait for that one. Maybe he'd send a big bouquet when she got back in her own house. Sort of a welcome-back-home gesture.

He knocked on the door, even though Tyler had given him the security code and he could have bypassed the system like one of the family. Tonight needed to be more formal, though, Calen thought, feeling like a teenager on his first date.

Tyler was the one to swing the door open. Then he looked Calen up and down before giving him an approving nod.

"Looking good," the man said, as he stepped aside and motioned for Calen to come inside. "Mom will be right out."

"I can wait," Calen said as he stepped into the house. "Don't rush her."

Calen reached up to his collar again. He could hear the sound of female voices from a distance. He hoped her daughters-in-law weren't giving Gracie too much advice. Dating had changed a lot since he and Gracie were teenagers. There wasn't much this younger generation knew that would interest him and her.

Then the door opened and Calen just stood there.

The woman framed in the doorway looked like Gracie, but couldn't be.

"Your hair," Calen managed to say. He hadn't seen Gracie without her long braid in years. In fact, she'd worn her hair like that in high school when he'd met her. And now, a fluffy cloud of shiny black strands framed her face. The haircut was level with her chin, and the bangs hung wispy across her forehead. She could be on the cover of one of those glossy magazines the women liked at the beauty shop.

"You like it, right?" Tyler whispered as he stepped close from behind. His voice was low, but Calen heard him fine. "Angelina cut it for her."

Calen swallowed and said to Gracie, "Your hair is beautiful."

And then he realized. A woman like that would have no interest in an old rancher like him. That much about dating had stayed the same since high school.

Only then did Calen's eyes look down to the dress. He had no words left, so he pursed his lips into a quiet whistle. It would have been louder, but he didn't have the breath in him.

What had they done to his Gracie? They had moved her beyond his reach.

Oh, but she was a vision in the deep pink dress. Just as he'd pictured she would look with all of those roses around her. Only instead of petals, it was a smooth satin that covered her shoulders and cascaded down the front of her. The golden brown of her arms was lovely. Her skin soft.

She might be out of his league now, but he owed her the truth. He looked her right in the eyes and smiled.

"You're beautiful. Absolutely beautiful."

Everyone was silent for a minute.

Then Tyler cleared his throat.

"Oh." Calen stepped forward and held out the corsage. "I brought something for you."

"Ohhh." The sounds of the daughters-in-law reached Calen's ears.

"Good job," Tyler said quietly, still standing beside him.

"Do you think she likes it?" Calen asked. "I don't want to make her uncomfortable."

The young women had exclaimed over the roses as if they were rock-size diamonds, but Gracie hadn't said anything. She'd just stood there as though she didn't know what to do.

"She'll get used to it," Tyler said, amusement in his voice.

The big question was whether he would get used to her, Calen realized.

He was glad he'd left the diamond ring in the glove compartment of the sedan. He had bought it today in a wild impulse of hope. The manager of the store had said he could return it with no questions asked, and Calen realized now what a kindness that was.

Just then he saw Tessie peek out from behind Gracie's skirt. The toddler had a pink ribbon wrapped around her head and a grin on her face. Calen consoled himself with the thought that life still held good things for a man like him. His granddaughter didn't look at him with fear in her eyes. She wasn't running to him in welcome, but maybe she'd come to like him. He only hoped Gracie wasn't going to leave both of them behind before she found out how sweet life could be if they all just trusted each other.

Chapter Fourteen

Gracie couldn't get used to her hair. Every time she looked down, it fell into her eyes and made her blink. Unfortunately, as the sky darkened and Calen drove them steadily toward the church in Dry Creek, she felt the urge to look down more and more often. Why hadn't her family told her that the neckline on this dress plunged like Niagara Falls when she was seated? It was way too deep for a woman of her age.

"Trouble?" Calen asked, as he turned to look at her.

The car was dark inside, but he could still see her movements, just as she could see his.

"No, ah," Gracie muttered as she squared her shoulders. "I'm fine."

She needed to keep a military bearing and her neckline would stay in place. And Amy had put a nice white shawl in her arms as she'd left the house. She could always wrap that around her.

"I thought maybe you lost an earring," Calen said.

Gracie shook her head. "I just have the necklace."

"I noticed it. Very nice."

Gracie smiled. "My boys gave it to me."

He nodded, but didn't say anything more.

In fact, now that she thought about it, he'd been particularly quiet since he'd picked her up. She wondered if he was worried she might not understand about the corsage. She knew it was in gratitude for all the help she'd given him with his granddaughter. She looked over at his profile. He didn't need to worry she'd read more into it than that.

She turned to the window and looked at the passing fields. Dusk had grown to full darkness, but she could still see the fence posts beside the road. Unless she missed her guess, the ground would see frost again tonight. And that was fine. The harvest was all gathered and the land was at rest. She glanced into the backseat and saw that Tessie still had a fierce grip on her new doll.

"That was nice of you to get something

for Tessie," Gracie said then. "It's—ah—quite large."

Calen turned to her and smiled. "I wasn't sure, but I thought maybe it would make her feel safer to have a big doll to sleep with instead of the little one. You know, someone to help fight against the night monsters with her."

"Actually, that makes sense," Gracie said in surprise. She wasn't used to a man who was so thoughtful of others. Buck had never tried to see life through the eyes of their sons, especially when they were so young.

Calen made the turn onto the gravel road that led into Dry Creek.

"We all need to feel safe." He looked up at the rearview mirror. "That's why I hope Tessie learns to trust me."

Gracie could see him watching his granddaughter, and his wistfulness stirred something in her. "I'm sure she will soon. You've been very nice to her."

"Of course. She's family."

Gracie nodded, and almost said something. Then she decided not to spoil any part of the evening by telling him about her sons and their feelings toward their father. There would be time for that later if he was interested.

Before Gracie knew it, Calen was parking the car alongside the asphalt near the church.

The moon was rising and there were stars in the night sky. Several families were already climbing the stairs together, and she could see their silhouettes against the light inside the church as they opened the door. Either the father or the mother was carrying a dish of food. Over the years, some women had brought the same food to the potlucks often enough to be noted for it.

Mrs. Hargrove always made enough of her baking-powder biscuits to go around with a healthy scoop of her homemade chokecherry jelly. Mrs. Redfern made a spicy rice dish that was popular. The men from the Elkton Ranch usually brought several big, slow-cooked roasts. The pastor and his wife made lemonade. Doris June brought chicken enchiladas.

"My sons and their wives are bringing pies this year," Gracie said as Calen opened his door. "Chocolate. Lemon. And blueberry. They're from the whole Stone family."

She wasn't sure she would have dared to make anything for the potluck herself, so she was glad she had been able to work with her daughters-in-law. Spaghetti was the only dish she made really well, and it would be difficult to bring that to a potluck without overcooking the noodles.

Calen opened her door and then turned to do the same for Tessie's.

"You shouldn't be carrying her tonight," Calen said. "You have your high heels, and that dress is satin. If she has sticky fingers, it'll stain. I'm going to see if she'll come to me."

Just then, Gracie saw a county car pull up next to them and stop.

Sheriff Wall rolled down his window and leaned out. "Just who I wanted to see. Do you have a child seat in the car?"

"Of course," Calen said as he turned to face the officer.

Sheriff Wall opened his door and stepped out. He was wearing a brown suit and tie instead of his uniform.

"I can't believe you're stopping people to ask about child seats," Gracie said to the lawman as she stepped out of the car. "At this time of night when we're all going to church."

Sheriff Wall paused in midstride to look at her and shake his head. "You're never going to trust me, are you, Gracie?"

She crossed her arms. "I don't know."

The sheriff grinned at her and continued on his way. "Nice dress, by the way."

The lawman stopped in front of Calen. "Good job with the corsage, too. I heard you two were on the big date. I've been praying it goes well for you."

Gracie wasn't sure what she thought of that remark. She was hardly against prayer, but somehow it didn't sit well that people thought Calen would need that much help managing a date with her.

The lawman just kept looking at Calen, though.

"We finally got that Denny Hampton to talk," he said. "Turns out Denny stashed a good bit of the robbery money in an old gym locker in Havre. He figured Carter Benson is looking for the key to that locker, and that's why he stole the Kewpie doll from Tessie in the first place when he left them to go east. Denny made the mistake of telling him that the key always went with the girl, so he figured it had to be inside the doll."

Gracie looked at the toddler in horror. "Why, he could have kidnapped her!"

"I'm sure he wished he had," the sheriff said with a nod. "But I've been all over the car and everything that was in it trying to find that key. Then it occurred to me. You took that child seat out of the car, and Carter never had a chance to search it."

"I'll get Tessie," Gracie said. She didn't care if her dress got wrinkled or stained. She wasn't going to leave that sweet girl anywhere near something that bad man wanted.

Calen was already unbuckling the straps before Gracie could open her arms.

When the girl was in Gracie's arms, Calen tipped the child's seat upside down. No one could see anything in the darkness, so the sheriff unhooked his flashlight and turned it on.

"There it is," Calen said, as he pulled back a bit of the vinyl edging on the side and showed the tip of a brass key to them all.

The sheriff pulled a plastic glove out of his pocket and slipped the key out of its hiding place.

"Denny also told us that Renee didn't know anything about the key," the lawman said. "He also confessed that he had forced her into that last robbery by threatening to hurt Tessie."

"The bully!" Gracie exclaimed as she tightened her grip on the toddler.

The sheriff nodded. "We still need to have a hearing, but Renee will be out on bail tomorrow for sure, and I'm guessing she's only going to be looking at some community service and probation."

Everyone was quiet for a minute.

"Thank you, Sheriff," Calen said. Then he

bowed his head, and Gracie knew he was saying a quick prayer of thanks.

"I'm sorry I gave you a hard time," Gracie said, turning to the sheriff.

Sheriff Wall shook his head as he looked at her and said softly, "No apology needed. Not from you."

Then he turned and walked over to the church. Gracie glanced up to the top of the stairs and saw that the sheriff's wife and children were waiting for him.

"He's a good man," Gracie said, looking over at Calen. "I keep forgetting that."

"We all need to remember a lot of things," Calen replied as he walked over to her, and put his arm around her shoulder. Before they could take a step, though, Tessie squirmed until her arm was free.

"Dolly!" she pointed to the backseat and demanded. Then she scrunched up her face until it got red.

"Okay," Calen said, sheepishly reaching into the car and bringing out the doll. He tucked it into his arm and looked at Gracie. "Am I spoiling her?"

"That's what grandparents do," Gracie said diplomatically.

Calen positioned the doll on his hip, much as Gracie was carrying her charge. Then he put an arm around her to keep her steady. Together they walked over to the steps leading up to the church.

The light in the foyer of the church was dim, and dozens of coats and jackets were hanging from the hooks on the far side. The ground was dry outside, so there was no mud inside. One child's forgotten overshoe sat under the bench.

"Mrs. Hargrove is gathering her class together in their Sunday-school area for a quick review for the skit," Calen reported as he opened the door for them to go down the stairs. "I had a phone call about it earlier today. We're to take Tessie."

Gracie gathered the shawl around her so she could protect her dress in case the toddler decided to rest against her. She'd forgotten about Tessie's nap today.

When they walked into the main room in the basement, Gracie saw that the tables had been decorated with the flowers the women of the church had made at Angelina's house the day before. Tissue flowers of every autumn color were scattered up and down a dozen rectangular tables. White sheets served as tablecloths. In the midst of the flowers, foil-wrapped chocolate kisses were scattered around.

"Smells good." Calen stopped and took an appreciative breath.

The women of the church were in the kitchen, and their voices could be heard. The men were gathered together in the far corner, assembling the cardboard pieces of Noah's ark.

"I better take Tessie back to Mrs. Hargrove," Gracie said as she started to walk in the right direction. "I might stay and help her get the kids organized, too."

"Not without me," Calen muttered as he followed. "I'm not standing out in the middle here with nothing but a doll in my arms. Not after everybody knows we're supposed to be on a date."

"Oh," Gracie said, stopping and turning to look at him. Then she grinned. "They'd think I jilted you."

"And before dinner, too," Calen agreed grimly. "It certainly wouldn't do my reputation any good. And the doll would make me look, well, pathetic."

Gracie chuckled and heard Calen join in. It wasn't every man who could laugh at himself, she thought in surprise.

Gracie pulled back the black curtain when she got to the right area and was greeted by a lion's roar. The roaring child took his mask off, and it turned out to be the prison boy.

"Scary," Gracie muttered in approval. "David, right? David Drake?"

Gracie had made a point to learn the children's names after that Sunday-school disaster.

The boy nodded, clearly pleased. He wrapped the brown blanket more closely around him, and it did almost look like lion's fur.

"Good costume," Calen added.

Tessie squirmed, indicating she wanted to be set down, and Gracie obliged. Mrs. Hargrove had just finished tying a dove mask on the timid rabbit girl.

"There you go, Lizzie," Mrs. Hargrove said as she patted the girl on her head. "Just remember to coo."

"Where's Timmy?" the girl demanded, and turned until she saw the boy who had tormented her in class. She walked over to him and thrust out another dove mask. "Here. Put this on."

"I don't want to be a stupid bird," the boy muttered.

"Deal with it," the girl said in a voice that, except for being several octaves higher and many degrees cuter, had the same inflection as Calen's when he'd told them the same thing.

Gracie applauded the girl's bravery, but she did so silently because the truce between the two children seemed fragile. She did see the girl glance over at Calen, though, and smile when he gave her a discreet thumbs-up.

Mrs. Hargrove turned then and saw Gracie and Calen. "Oh, there you are!"

The older woman's face was so serene her eyes were sparkling even before she smiled at them. "I'm so thankful you got the children organized. It would be chaos if they hadn't had a chance to practice on Sunday."

"We only really got them paired up," Gracie confessed as she looked around. "They obey you a lot better than they did us."

"That's because I always have lemon drops in my pockets," the older woman said, and then she focused on Gracie. "I know the women want to talk to you in the kitchen. They have something to ask you and they haven't had a chance."

Mrs. Hargrove turned to Calen. "You don't mind, do you? It'll just be a minute, and I'm afraid there won't be time after we eat, and then the program starts. And if the women don't get a chance to have their say, they won't be able to sit back and enjoy the program later."

Gracie looked up at Calen in panic. There wasn't anything he could do, but she could see from his eyes that he wanted to try.

"I'm not sure we, ah, have time," Calen finally stumbled through enough words that Gracie hoped she was saved. "We have to, ah, cut the pie. Yes, the Stones brought a lot of pies, and they all need to be cut."

"Nonsense," Mrs. Hargrove said, and it was clear that she ruled in this room. "You can cut the pies and listen to the women at the same time."

"I don't want to leave Calen with the doll," Gracie said.

Mrs. Hargrove frowned at that, as she seemed to finally notice the doll in Calen's arms. "That's awful big for Tessie." Then she brightened. "But it will make her feel good at night."

"That's what I thought," Calen said, and Gracie could tell he was weakening.

"Maybe you should leave the doll here," Mrs. Hargrove suggested. "We might be able to use it in the march to the ark. We don't have even numbers, you know."

"I don't think Noah took any dolls on board," Gracie said, feeling a little surly.

Mrs. Hargrove just clucked her tongue. "Of course not. But this is pretend."

Gracie decided to give up. "I'll go talk to the women in the kitchen."

She turned to go and was surprised when she noticed Calen walking beside her.

"You don't need to do this," she said as they crossed the floor of the main room.

"I'm your date," Calen said a little grimly. "I wouldn't let you go into a war zone by yourself. So I won't let you go into that kitchen."

"Thank you," Gracie said.

She looked to check, and the men were all preoccupied trying to get the final wall of the ark put into place. There was no one else around.

"I'm not used to this kind of chivalry," Gracie said.

"Well, you should be."

That's when she drew herself up to her full height in that old prom dress and did what she should have done decades ago. She kissed Calen right on the lips. She was shorter than him and she knew she'd surprised him, so the kiss didn't have the force that it might have. But she felt it got her message across.

A big grin spread over Calen's face.

"You are one special guy," she said. "I'll always be grateful."

The sparkle in his eye dimmed as he looked at her. "Grateful?"

"Of course. Why?"

"No reason," he said.

Then he walked over and opened the kitchen door for her.

The warm, damp air hit Gracie in the face as she walked over the threshold.

"Mrs. Stone!" Mary, the Sunday-school teacher who never failed to recognize her, called a greeting from across the room. Everyone stopped to look. Gracie threw her shoulders back. Now wasn't the time for the neckline to be low.

"You're just the person we want to talk to," Mary said as she started walking over.

Gracie glanced to her side to make sure Calen was in place.

The single mother, Mrs. Drake, was looking at her intently, too.

"I am so sorry." Gracie repeated what she had said several days ago. She might as well cut to the heart of things. "I had no intention of mentioning prisons in Sunday school. I never told them anything they shouldn't know. And I'll never do anything like that again. I promise."

Gracie figured that should about cover it.

"But, of course, you need to do it again,"

Mary said in astonishment. "That's what we're trying to tell you."

Gracie blinked. "You are?"

She looked over at Calen, but he looked stunned, too.

"You see, it's my David," Mrs. Drake said as she twisted her hands. "He can't seem to get past prisons."

Well, Gracie had to agree with that.

"His father's serving time, you see," the boy's mother continued. "Back on the East Coast. I've taken David to see him once, but I can't afford to go every year, and there are no jobs back where we lived, so I couldn't stay."

"That's why we want you to talk to the Sunday-school children about what it's like to be in prison," Mary continued. "Nothing too harsh, you understand. But just enough so that they know God is with people in prisons, too. I know you had your Bible-study group, but we haven't heard much about it."

"Please say yes," Mrs. Drake continued. "David worries about his father, and if he knew how to pray for him, he might find some comfort."

Gracie was listening to the words, but her mind wasn't making sense of them.

"But I thought you didn't like me because

I've been to prison," she finally blurted it all out.

"Oh, dear, no," Mary said. "We just didn't want to bother you."

"You've had a lot to deal with," Mrs. Drake agreed.

"That's it?" Gracie asked in relief. "You just want me to talk about it?"

Mary nodded. "I believe so."

"Well, then, pick a Sunday you want me to come. I could maybe even work in some of Paul's experiences from the Bible," Gracie offered.

"That would be wonderful." Mary stood there beaming and then blushed as she looked down.

Gracie looked down, too, just in time to see Calen's hand finally grab hold of hers.

"And that's such a lovely corsage," Mrs. Drake said a little wistfully as she turned to go back to the stove. "So romantic."

"I'm sure you'll have a wonderful evening," Mary gushed, and she, too, turned to leave.

Gracie just stood there for a minute, and then she looked over at Calen. "They like me."

"Of course." He held her hand as they walked back into the main room. "How could they not? You're strong. Kindhearted. Beautiful."

Gracie just shook her head. "Flatterer."

Calen drew her hand closer to him. "A man's entitled to his opinion."

She wasn't so sure about that, she thought as she studied his profile. But then she decided a woman was entitled to her views on a man as well. And she was warming toward this one. In fact, she probably had been since high school.

Chapter Fifteen

Gracie settled back into her folding chair after eating a piece of chocolate pie for dessert. Golden light from fluorescent tubes reached into the corners of the basement. The aroma from the food stirred the air even though almost every dish had been scraped clean. Tables had been cleared and women had folded their aprons, setting them on a shelf next to the sink.

Gracie looked across the room and saw the friendly faces of her neighbors. She was at home here tonight in a way she hadn't been since she'd come back from prison. And she owed most of that to Calen.

Funny, witty, warm-hearted Calen. He'd been the perfect companion tonight, building bridges between her and her neighbors so they could discover the many things they shared. She hadn't realized until she watched him talk how easy it had been for her to build walls around herself and assume that people's awkwardness was hostility toward her instead of just discomfort.

And now Calen was standing in line at the front of the room where the pulpit had been set up. Tradition had it that, at the harvest dinner, anyone in Dry Creek who wanted to do so could stand up and announce what their work had brought forth during the past year. It was a time of accounting and was intended to mark progress in personal as well as ranching goals.

She remembered Buck going up a time or two, early in their marriage when he still allowed a few public events. He had liked to mark his successes, and she had been pleased for him that he could boast of a few, although her heart had stung the year he'd bragged about all he'd done that year and hadn't even mentioned that Wade had been born.

Elmer finished telling about the addition he had built onto his house, and Calen was walking over to the pulpit.

"I've been the ranch foreman at the Elkton place, off and on, for over twenty years now," Calen said as he braced his hands against the wood and leaned forward. "Ranching is hard work, but everyone here knows that. What I've been learning lately, though, is that growing crops isn't nearly as hard or as important as growing good, honest children."

Several murmurs of agreement were heard across the room.

"I'm here tonight because I want to say in front of everyone that I'm grateful God is giving me a second chance now to be a father and a grandfather. I'll admit I don't know much about doing either, so I'll be asking for your advice and prayers. Most of you know my daughter, Renee, got mixed up in those robberies up north. I take most of the blame for that, because I didn't tell her often enough that she could come to me with any problem that she had."

Calen paused for a moment.

"That's a mistake I mean to correct. I'm hoping she gets out on bail soon, so we can both work at being a family. And taking care of my granddaughter. You've probably seen little Tessie around with me and Gracie. The girl needs to learn how to trust men, and I need to learn how to trust God to help me be the grandfather she needs."

A sound of muffled laughter came from behind Gracie, and she turned. It came from the stairwell where Tessie and the other toddlers were gathered, receiving final instructions on how to make their journey to the ark memorable. Many a humpbacked blanket had made a brief appearance out of the stairwell earlier this evening before being called back inside. The door was firmly closed now, and the laughter settled down.

Before long, Calen walked back and sat down beside Gracie. She put her hand on his arm without thinking about it. She had been slowly realizing how different Calen was from her late husband, and this evening confirmed it. Where Buck boasted of what he had done, Calen asked for help to do better. While Buck had thought of his success, Calen thought of his family.

She leaned close to him while the next person walked up to the microphone.

"How do you feel about the color orange?" she asked in a whisper.

"I can live without it," he whispered back, his eyes dancing with amusement. "Why? Are you going to buy me a tie or something?"

She shook her head. "I'm just wondering who you think should make the decorating decisions in a family? Father? Mother? Kids?"

His eyes stopped smiling. "You're serious?"

She didn't say anything. She wasn't sure how serious she was.

"I think people can work these things out,"

he finally said to her, his voice low and filled with emotion. "A little compromise here and a little compromise there. Most people aren't as far apart as they think."

Gracie nodded and smiled. She noticed people had seen her whisper a few things to Calen, and they were nodding at her in encouragement. If she did trust a man again, it would have to be someone like the one sitting right here beside her. Maybe in a year or two, she would be ready.

Calen kept his eyes on the pulpit as the pastor's wife talked. He heard something about an art program she had taught for disadvantaged youths. It was all very good, but his mind was racing too fast to listen.

Something had happened in Gracie's heart. He could tell by the way she relaxed her shoulders around him and leaned a little toward him instead of away from him. He'd studied his granddaughter's face so often lately that he recognized the signs of growing trust in Gracie.

Lord, do we have a chance? he asked.

He couldn't rush Gracie, but he wanted to.

She leaned close to him then and whispered, "See the doves coming?"

The girl and the boy were flying low coming out of the stairwell and going toward the ark, but they were making it work together. The boy was taller, so he would swoop down when he passed the girl, and she would raise her arms at the same angle to pass him. Their bird masks firmly on their heads, they danced and swayed all the way up to the front of the room, where Noah magically appeared to let them inside the ark.

"And they do have bars on the windows," Gracie whispered.

"I think that's only so the cardboard doesn't collapse," Calen said. "No one really knows."

Gracie grinned and then shrugged.

The doves stood guard as the lions made their way up and into the ark. And then the sheep came, holding hands and bleating.

"Very romantic," Calen ventured to say, and Gracie looked as if she was trying not to smile as she nodded.

Most of the animals were standing next to the ark when the teenage helpers walked by, gray blankets over their backs and hoses of some kind swinging this way and that.

"I don't think Mrs. Hargrove had them in the lineup," Gracie said with a slight frown.

"Who can resist being part of the show?" Calen asked.

Then his forehead furrowed, too. And he counted the children that were in the ark.

"Shouldn't Tessie be out there?" he asked.

Gracie turned around to look at the door to the stairwell. "She was a turtle, so she was coming last."

The stairway door was propped open, but no little girl came out. Calen frowned as he looked around. "Don't tell me Tessie is back there alone?"

He started to stand. All the children and helpers were in the room except Tessie. There was a loud screech from the stairwell and Tessie came running through the door, her toddler legs going as fast as they could. Her turtle mask was hanging from one ear and her blond curls were bouncing all over each other. Calen was out of his chair when he realized he would only scare her more if he moved toward her. She was running straight to Gracie, who was the one she turned to for comfort, and he moved out of the way to make her trip easier.

But Tessie wasn't headed for Gracie. Her little legs changed course when he moved and they took her right to him, and she put her arms up. He swooped down and lifted her to him as she wrapped her arms around his neck and whispered, "Bad man."

"What?" Calen froze.

"Bad man," Tessie repeated, and this time she turned and pointed to the stairway door.

"Carter?" Calen whispered.

Tessie nodded. "At the top of the stairs. But I runned in here."

Calen looked over to where Sheriff Wall had been sitting, but the lawman had heard and was already halfway over to the stairwell, along with a couple of the Stone boys as well.

Calen started to hand Tessie to Gracie so he could go with the other men, but Tessie held tight to his neck.

"The sheriff and my sons will catch him," Gracie whispered to him. "Don't worry about that."

"The fool. I suppose he thought Tessie had that key on her somehow."

Calen sat down with Tessie still wrapped tight around him. He could feel her still trembling and he rubbed her back as he'd seen Gracie do to soothe her.

Gracie looked over at the man with his granddaughter and burst into prayer. *Thank You, Father.*

Then she noticed how Calen's hands gently reminded Tessie that she was safe with him.

An unexpected longing shot through her, and she blinked back a tear. She wasn't sure she could wait a year to have someone love her like that again.

But Calen had forgotten about her. He had his family in his arms.

Gracie's heart broke a little, but life went on. She heard the sounds of boots going up and down the basement stairs. A few of the women had joined hands and were praying. The animals in the ark were talking.

And then Calen lifted his face and looked at her squarely.

"Come," he said as he opened his arms wide enough to include her.

Gracie didn't hesitate. She leaned into his embrace and was part of the circle.

"I love you," Calen whispered in her ear. "And I realize I can't wait. I want a second chance at happiness. And I want it with you."

"I love you, too," Gracie said, as her voice wavered.

Then he kissed her. Gracie scarcely heard the applause that went up from the friends around her when it happened.

"I want a second chance, too," she had presence of mind enough to whisper when Calen pulled away.

She looked down and Calen, with Tessie still in his arms, was kneeling like a man half his age.

"Will you marry me, Gracie?" he asked as he held a hand up for hers.

"I—" she started, then hesitated.

"Trust me," he said then.

She looked in his eyes as she put her hand in his, realizing he was a man who would protect her as readily as he had his granddaughter. "I do trust you."

"So you'll marry me?" His eyes were more serious now than she'd ever seen them.

She nodded.

The basement was silent for a moment and then the applause began.

Calen stood and leaned down to press his lips to hers again. Gracie kissed him back with every hope and every dream she had in her heart. She trusted this man with everything she was.

Neither one of them noticed that the clapping got even louder.

Epilogue

Five weeks later, Gracie stood at the back of the Dry Creek church and looked at the mauve carpet that went from her feet straight to the altar at the front. She was ready to walk the bridal path. Tessie had already walked down the aisle scattering the rose petals from the basket her grandfather had given her earlier. There were white petals, red petals and pink petals. There were, however, no petals that were even close to orange.

She smiled. Calen had helped her pick out the colors and decorations for her bedroom, and she'd been staying at Tyler's until the work was done. She wanted to share the first night in the room with Calen. They planned to live there.

Mrs. Hargrove was at the piano and she struck up the chords to the bridal march.

Gracie blinked as she looked down the path and saw Calen standing there in a black tuxedo. He had said he wanted to match the finery of the ivory lace dress that she wore. She'd bought the dress because the beading on the fitted bodice matched the string of beautiful pearls her sons had given to her. Everything revolved around family for her now.

Her sons were lined up next to her. Wade was on one side and Jake and Tyler on the other. For weeks, they had squabbled about which one of them was going to walk her down the aisle, until Calen had stepped into the fray. He told them firmly that they were brothers and they needed to find a compromise. When they couldn't seem to, he suggested they all walk down the aisle together and give her away in harmony.

That seemed to work for them, Gracie thought. Her sons were happier, now that they had someone to fill a father role in their lives at times.

Gracie took a deep breath and signaled her sons that it was time to walk forward.

With her eyes on her groom, Gracie didn't pay much attention to whether her boys kept pace with her. Calen was smiling all the while she kept walking.

When she and her sons reached the front of

the church, her boys went to the side and stood where bridesmaids normally would. Renee had chosen to be at the front with Calen and took the best-man place. It was all reversed, but it worked.

Renee's bruises were healed, and the courts had decided she was a victim rather than a criminal in all that had happened. She had taken the job as cook for the Elkton bunkhouse and was living in the quarters there with Tessie. Sheriff Wall had caught Carter Benson the night of the harvest dinner, and the man had turned out to be helpful as he'd grudgingly made a statement that before he had left, Danny had terrorized Renee.

Gracie and Calen held hands as they faced the pastor with their family gathered around them. Together they had changed the vows to reflect their love. Calen had said he didn't want Gracie to obey him; he wanted her to trust him instead. She was ready to promise that.

When the vows were over, the pastor presented them to the congregation. The church had never seen as much whooping and hollering as it did that day. Even the reporter that had come to church to take Gracie's photo was there. He'd offered to be the official wedding photographer and promised to leak only one picture, which Gracie chose, to the press. She'd decided it wouldn't hurt the whole state to see her happy, so she'd agreed.

After a few family photos in front of the church, everyone went down to the basement where the women of the church had laid out a buffet of salads and breads. They had insisted Gracie let them help with the reception, and she had learned her lesson. She accepted with gratitude, knowing they were offering their friendship as well.

When the cake was all gone and the gifts opened, the bride and groom slipped away to make one last stop before they left.

"It's a nice, solid stone," Calen said as they viewed the marker that had just been put in place over Buck's grave the day before.

Gracie nodded. She knew how much effort her sons had made to have the marker there before her wedding. In the end, there had been no clever words for the final resting place of her late husband.

She had left the decision to her boys, and they had settled on putting their father's full name and the dates of his birth and death. They considered his ties to the ranch that was dear to all of their hearts. It had been his legacy to them. Underneath his name they had chiseled in granite the full text of Matthew 5:45: "He causes His sun to rise on the wicked and the good, and He makes it rain on the just and the unjust."

Gracie had not known the words they would choose until now. "They left it all in God's hands."

Buck nodded. "They're smart boys."

Then the two of them turned as one to walk back to the church. Calen put his arm around Gracie. "It'll be good to go home."

She nodded. She was ready to begin her new life with Calen. God had given her a second chance at love and she'd be forever grateful. Then she looked up at her husband and smiled.

"I do love you," she whispered.

He bent to kiss her. "I love you, too."

* * * * *

Dear Reader,

I hope you have enjoyed the final book in this RETURN TO DRY CREEK series. The Stone family will always have a place in my heart, particularly Gracie, and I hope she has touched your heart as well. When she made the ultimate sacrifice for her sons, because she felt responsible for not removing the boys from their abusive father, I felt the indecision right along with her. I am sure many mothers have the same kinds of fears and regrets that Gracie had.

For that reason, I dedicated this book to broken families. I know some of you reading these pages have experienced the troubles of the Stone family in your own lives. Because of that, I pray these books can be of some comfort to you. I firmly believe we have reason to hope in God, no matter what the situation may be. He loves us.

And, be assured, I will be working on happily-ever-after for Calen's daughter, Renee, and her daughter, Tessie.

If you have a minute, I'd love to hear from you. Just contact me through my website at www.janettronstad.com. In the meantime, may God bless you and keep you in His love. Sincerely yours,

Janet Tronstad

Questions for Discussion

1. What do you think of Gracie Stone's decision to go to prison to protect the son she believes is guilty of murder? Why do you think she did it? Would you ever do something like that? How do you think God sees such an act? Is it wrong for being a lie, or is it noble for being selfless?

2. Gracie believes the women in the church do not accept her because of the time she spent in prison. Would you feel differently about an ex-con in your church versus a soccer mom?

3. Gracie's sons believe their mother needs to get married. Their advice to her was clearly unwanted. What do you do with unwanted advice? When should we listen to such advice anyway?

4. Gracie opens the door at night to help someone in need. We live in a world where it is often dangerous to help others. Have you ever been put in a situation where you wanted to help, but were afraid? What did you do? What do you think Gracie should have done that night?

5. Gracie and Calen knew each other once, but they grew apart. Why do you think they did so? Did they feel guilty? Awkward? As though they were betraying Buck Stone if they were friends? What would you do if you were one of those characters?

6. When Mrs. Hargrove has her husband ask Gracie to substitute for her as Sunday-school teacher, Gracie panics. Gracie wants to refuse, but she owes Mrs. Hargrove. Do you think people should ever teach Sunday-school out of a sense of obligation? Have you ever been asked to do something that you felt you should even though you dreaded it? What did you do?

7. The Stone boys finally were able to think of something to write on their father's headstone. Have you ever had to write something pleasant about someone whom you had a conflict with (a Christmas card, perhaps, or a eulogy)? Is it best to tell the unvarnished truth or give a softer version for the public, families and others?

8. Gracie realizes she did not stand up to her abusive husband and she should have, even

over something as simple as the color of the walls. If you were to give Gracie and her husband marital counseling early in their marriage, what would you say to them?

LARGER-PRINT BOOKS!

**GET 2 FREE
LARGER-PRINT NOVELS
PLUS 2 FREE
MYSTERY GIFTS**

Larger-print novels are now available...

Love Inspired ®
SUSPENSE
RIVETING INSPIRATIONAL ROMANCE

Watch for our series of edge-
of-your-seat suspense novels.
These contemporary tales
of intrigue and romance
feature Christian characters
facing challenges to their faith...
and their lives!

AVAILABLE IN REGULAR
& LARGER-PRINT FORMATS

For exciting stories that reflect traditional values,
visit:

www.ReaderService.com

LISUSDIR11B